MW01134320

The Chalk Giant

CHRISTOPHER GREAVES

Bloomington, IN Milton Keynes, UK

AuthorHouse™
1663 Liberty Drive, Suite 200
Bloomington, IN 47403
www.authorhouse.com
Phone: 1-800-839-8640

AuthorHouse™ UK Ltd.
500 Avebury Boulevard
Central Milton Keynes, MK9 2BE
www.authorhouse.co.uk
Phone: 08001974150

First published by AuthorHouse 6/14/2006

ISBN: 1-4259-3897-3 (sc)

Printed in the United States of America
Bloomington, Indiana

This book is printed on acid-free paper.

For George and Raphael

My thanks to Darin Jewell

The Dancing Man

In the summer of my fourteenth year, towards the very end of childhood, I saw something which changed all our lives.

We were out for a walk, Dad, Clara, and I. I'd gone ahead, half-running, half-slithering down the chalk path which led from the top of Woodcote Hill. Now I was resting on the stile at the bottom. My father, equipped with a panama hat, and my sister, who'd just reached that age when you begin to be self-conscious about running down hills, were still making their way down the path towards me.

I remember watching them, just watching them, while whatever the thoughts I'd been thinking receded and my mind grew transparent, like glass. I seemed to see, not my father and my sister, but two figures whom I'd never seen before, two figures who might have stepped out of an Impressionist painting, the one in a panama hat and the other in a dress of green lawn.

I shifted my gaze to the hill itself. Now, what is called 'Woodcote Hill' is really three hills put together. The outer two spurs, which sloped fairly gently down to the field beside me, were patched and dotted with scrub and pine trees, but the hill in the middle, which was steeper, was bare of bushes and trees, being covered only with grass, emblazoned here and there with yellow specks of St John's Wort and Bird's Foot Trefoil, and scribbled upon with the

1

short black stumps of hawthorn trees burnt in a fire a few years back. It was on this central part that my eyes were fixed.

It had been the driest summer for many, many years. It hadn't rained for weeks, and in places the grass on the Surrey Hills was the colour of straw. It was like that on Woodcote Hill. It looked as though the carpet of grass had been turned upside down, revealing the hessian backing beneath.

So there I was, staring up at the dry, shorn hill in a moment of calm abstraction, when all of a sudden I noticed something odd about it - something exceptionally odd which I'd never once seen before.

The westering sun was casting a wonderfully golden light on the short, brownish grass: a light in which everything seemed much more sharply defined than usual. Assisted by this evening sunlight and perhaps by my run down the hill, my eyesight became like a hawk's: I saw the hill before me with a clear-eyed, startling intensity. And what I saw in particular was a *shape* - a peculiar beneath or on the surface of the golden grass.

It was very faint, and had the sun not been shining at just that angle, and had the grass not been so dry, and had I not been sitting just where I was, alone at the foot of the hill, I might never have seen it. But I did see it, and the more I gazed, the more distinct the shape became.

There was a sort of huge, jagged circle, and within this circle was the figure of a man, a man who might have been dancing.

I shut my eyes for a moment, then looked again. It was still there, crystallising before me. I turned away and glanced across the curving face of the Downs to the right, and then to the left and the thick wooded slopes of the Buckland Hills. Then I looked back once more.

There was nothing there.

No, wait - there was! But it was like a puzzle picture, or like a face in the clouds in a picture in one of our school books. You either saw it or you didn't. And if you didn't see it at first, it could take you a long time before you did - while the rest of the boys stood around saying, "What, can't you see it *yet*? But it's *obvious*," etc, etc.

I called out to my sister and father.

"Clara! Dad!"

They heard me, but didn't alter their casual pace. "Dad! *Daddy!*" I shouted, the way I still did when I was excited.

Maddeningly, instead of coming on faster my father merely paused and looked towards me. I signalled with a kind of desperation. I was very aware that as the sun sank lower, this vision of the dancing man would probably disappear, and I really wanted Dad to see it, for Dad, I knew, would be interested. Clara too, for that matter. But Dad - yes, Dad would be *particularly* interested.

At last he began to respond to my frantic waving and came on more hurriedly. Clara, who had got to that age when you don't necessarily come running when your little brother calls, was hanging back. At least, I *think* she was hanging back, but she may have been in a dream. That was quite possible. Anyway, I remember thinking that, really, it would be quicker to go and get Dad and drag him to where I was, but - superstitiously, perhaps - I didn't want to leave my position for fear that, when on my return, this strange dancing man would be gone.

Finally, my father reached me.

"Yes, what is it?"

I pointed at the hill. "Look."

Dad looked. I dare say he knew that I must mean something and wouldn't be wasting his time or playing a joke, but he couldn't know what he was supposed to be looking *at*.

I could tell from his concerned yet placid expression that he hadn't yet seen the dancing figure in its circle, but I didn't want to lead the witness, as they say in court. I wanted him to see it for himself - partly to confirm that the ghostly, mysterious figure really did exist.

"Look there - on the hill. *In* the hill," I said quietly.

There was a pause, a long pause which could not have lasted more than five seconds but which seemed to me to last about five minutes, and then all of a sudden my father tensed up with excitement.

"Oh my *goodness!*" he exclaimed.

"Can you see it?"

"I certainly can. I certainly can. There's a vast man, he must be a hundred and fifty feet high - "

"And - "

"And a circle - broken at the bottom, but I'd say it's meant to be a circle - and it runs all around him. My goodness, my goodness - it's *Shiva*. It must be! Clara! Come and look at this..."

Almost hurrying now, Clara came up and followed Dad's gaze.

"Do you see it? Do you see the figure carved on the hill?"

Clara frowned. "I *think* so..."

But a moment later the light of the descending sun was interrupted by a clump of trees on rising ground to the west, and Woodcote Hill was cast into shadow. The ghostly dancing figure vanished.

"It's gone," I stated. "But what exactly *was* it, Dad?"

"What was it? Well, if you mean, 'What kind of a phenomenon was it,' it's been known for a goodish while that in prolonged dry spells - not that we have many of them in England - the traces of ancient field systems or, say, abandoned villages can begin to appear like shadows on the present landscape. Usually, they're more easily seen from the air - and tomorrow I'll call the Heritage Department and get them to send a plane over. This is incredible! Absolutely incredible! We must get photographic confirmation of this as soon as possible. Now, where was I? Yes, this figure - this figure of Shiva - must have been cut into the chalk of this hill, just like the Long Man of Wilmington in Sussex, or the Uffington White Horse. And it must have been done, oh, hundreds and hundreds or, much more probably, *thousands* of years ago."

Clara was still staring quizzically at the hill, though there was nothing to be seen there now but the dry brown grass and a few white scars of chalk.

"But how come we never knew it was here?" she said.

"Because it hasn't been this dry for a long, long time," Dad replied.

"Well, yes, but there must have been *some* dry summers in the last hundred years or so."

"Ye-es. Actually there was a drought about fifteen years ago," said Dad. He paused for a moment, thinking. "But of course! The hill was covered in scrub then. Then about seven or eight years ago some picnickers started a fire - you remember? - and most of the scrub was burned away. And this is the first really long dry spell since then."

"I wonder if anyone else has noticed the figure?" I mused.

"Well, I shouldn't think so. We'd surely have heard about it if they had. You may not realise it, Dan, but this discovery - *your* discovery - is a *big thing* - a huge thing! It's of major historical importance! And what's more it's so *strange*...a figure of Shiva - I'm sure it's meant to be Shiva - a figure of Shiva right here in Surrey. It's extraordinary! It throws a new light on everything we know about the past. And I shall be the one who breaks it to an astonished world!'

He said this with high good humour, knowing full well that not all the world would be astonished, but with an underlying seriousness, too - for Dad was a lecturer in Ancient History at the University of London, so the significance of this find was perfectly clear to him. Besides,

I knew it had always been his dream to make some new discovery or to advance some groundbreaking theory - which was hardly the easiest thing to do when your field of study comprised the long dead past. And to have made such a radical discovery on his very own doorstep, and so unexpectedly - it must have seemed a miracle!

"Oh...this is a great day!" he cried, and, taking off his panama hat, span it up into the air - high up into the clear blue August evening sky - and caught it as it fell.

"Oh...*Dad*," said Clara. I could see that she felt happy for Dad, yet couldn't help feeling a little embarrassed too. It was a phase she was going through.

Meanwhile, I sat on the stile and thought of all the times I had walked on Woodcote Hill, and of all the times that others must have walked here too, and how, for centuries, this figure had been there beneath our feet, behind a veil of earth and grass and flowers, overlooking the Weald, inscribed in an eternal dance within a wheel of fire, ablaze with symbolic power, and how we hadn't known the slightest thing about it - not the slightest thing.

Anna Karenina

We now fast-forward to much more recent times.

That opening scene took place in 1995. It was now three years later, at breakfast, at home. We were all there: Mum, Dad, myself and Clara. Mum was reading a letter; Clara was drinking coffee; I was looking at the first page of a book we'd been set for European Lit.

"'*Happy families are all alike; every unhappy family is unhappy in its own way,*'" I read. "What on earth does that mean?"

"Oh, that's just Tolstoy," said Clara. She said it as though Tolstoy was a stick of rock with the name *TOLSTOY* running through it.

We all looked at Clara. Or at least, Mum and I did. Dad simply went on staring into space, while holding his cup of tea in both hands. He looked the way a musician looks when his eyes are fixed, yet glazed, and you know he's not actually seeing anything. He's not trying to. He's listening instead, and that's pretty much how it was with Dad. He was listening to the music of his thoughts, and the fact that that music was something slow and gloomy and no doubt in D Minor was only too plain to see.

Clara, meanwhile, didn't follow up her interesting observation with reference to *Anna Karenina*. It passed through my mind for a second that perhaps she had only said what she'd said in order to change the subject, for if one thing was true, it was that our family was not

9

particularly happy - and, interestingly enough, the way in which it wasn't happy was somewhat unusual, if not to say unique. So, maybe Clara, not wanting us to focus on the subject which, unwontedly, I'd raised, had instead tried to kill it dead.

I thought this for a moment, then dismissed it. Or rather, I didn't exactly dismiss it. Instead, I put it in the Pending file. The thing was, it was hard to tell what Clara really thought about anything. Her voice had become so blasé and weary and grainy that she managed to sound - whether speaking of the price of eggs or the chances of a Third World War - as though it all meant the same to her, and that wasn't much.

She hadn't always been like that. No, she hadn't always been like that, but she'd certainly changed a lot in the last three years. Gone, for example, was her liking for Mozart and Bach. Now all you heard when you passed her room - or even if you didn't pass her room, but lived within a five hundred yard radius of our house - was the bone-crunching beat of one of 'thrash metal rock messiah' Ronnie Bastard's in-your-face pop anthems. Gone too were the days of those tana lawn dresses; now she mostly wore denim or leather. And gone were the days of her fondness for summery greens and flower or paisley patterns; now she wore indigo, black, or dark blue, and colourful patterns were strictly out. As for her hair, what at a pinch you could once have called auburn had now been dyed red. And when I say 'red', I don't mean 'discreetly hennaed'. I mean a vivid poppy red.

Her first appearance (three weeks ago) with her hair so coloured had at least had the merit of rousing Dad from his trance - though, since it had only been to start a caustic, running joke (if joke it could be called) about how his daughter had at last revealed what he'd long suspected: viz., that she was an alien, and which included quips about how 'the alien' was settling in quite well, how 'the alien' seemed almost human at times, etc., etc., one could wonder if this was a good thing or not.

These days Clara was in her first, foundation year at Art School. The Art School in question was the Nork School of Art and Design, a few miles up the road. Because it was so near, and because the family finances didn't allow for her to rent her own place, she still lived at home - which was why, on this morning in June near the end of the summer term, she was having breakfast with us and not by herself in some damp, grotty bed-sit, or else together with a gang of fellow students in some ghastly shared flat with paper peeling from the walls and that smell of cooked cabbage that just won't go away.

It was Mum's opinion that, since she'd been at the Art School, she had "come under someone's influence". This was Mum's way of accounting for Clara's change of style - though, needless to say, it was a notion which Clara dismissed with contempt. And one could see her point of view. No-one likes to be thought of as 'being under someone's influence', or as being conditioned by whatever's in fashion, or as being defined by anything. People like to think that whatever they come up with is their own

11

startlingly original idea - and if people like to think that, then let them, say I.

All the same, Mum wasn't far off the mark in her diagnosis, as events were shortly to reveal.

Meanwhile, Mum was reading the local paper. It was a Thursday, and the job vacancy section was less meagre than usual on Thursdays. Not that Mum wanted a job - it was just that it was looking more and more as though she might have to take one. If she could get one.

Suddenly, something caught her eye. "Oh, I see Bryan Mandeville's been left some money. Quite a lot, too. His father's just died and...let's see...yes, he must have come into a tidy fortune."

"Typical," said Dad with a distinct lack of enthusiasm. "That's just typical."

Bryan Mandeville, who lived in Epsom - not far from us - had been one of Dad's colleagues. He had also been - and still was, I guess - Dad's particular bugbear. They had never exactly hit it off, and towards the end of Dad's time in the Ancient History Department they had almost come to blows. I suppose that they hadn't seen one another for a year or so now - except on one occasion when, shopping in Epsom and coming upon Bryan Mandeville in a delicatessen, my father had cut him dead, like a character in a Victorian novel - but I knew that the old animosity was there, on Dad's side at least.

At this point, Clara stood up, finished her cup of coffee, wriggled more deeply into her second-hand leather jacket (a size too large for her) and, muttering something which might have been "See you", left the room.

There was silence for a moment, then Mum spoke.

"You don't...you don't think she could be on drugs, do you?" she said, looking anxiously at Dad.

"I hope so," said Dad. "She doesn't eat and she certainly hasn't drunk the milk of human kindness lately, so what else is there to keep her going but drugs?"

He didn't mean it, of course. It was just his way of expressing himself. And if it sounded bitter, well, I suppose my father had good reason to be bitter - when you looked at the facts.

The Shower Of Rain

To begin with, it had seemed as though it was going to be so easy. All that Dad had had to do was to get visual evidence of the Chalk Giant's existence, and then, as it were, claim copyright on the discovery. After that, he would be able to organise a dig on the site, he would be able to write a book about his findings, he would be assured of his place as a lecturer (for the Education budget being what it was, there was always the danger of his being made redundant), he would get his face on the cover of *Ancient History* or whatever his favourite journal was - he might even be offered a professorship - and all the rest of it. In particular, it would spell sufficient material security for him to pursue his other career: the writing of poetry.

To tell you the truth, I hadn't read much of Dad's poetry, and what I had read seemed a little convoluted and intellectual, with nice bits here and there which weren't altogether integrated, if you know what I mean...but that may well have been because Dad had never felt quite able to *relax*. I won't go into his whole story because it would take a year and a day to get through, but you can take it as read that he hadn't had an easy time of it in his younger days, and this lecturing job, insecure though it was, had been his first big break. Or his first big *material* break, at least. But now to be known as the discoverer of the Chalk Giant of Woodcote Hill - that would not only make his name, it would also set him up for life. As I say, it would give him the basis to do what he really wanted to do: write lyrical, thoughtful poems and, who knows, even get them published.

I dare say all these things had gone through his mind, that night we found the Giant. At any rate, the next day he'd rung the Heritage Department in order to have some aerofilm taken of the site. This had proved to be much more difficult than he'd foreseen. Far from being greeted with rapture, his news had been met with disinterest, then incredulity. Then, when he'd finally convinced them that he was a qualified professional who knew what he was talking about and not some eccentric amateur with a bee in his bonnet, he'd found himself getting enmeshed in the Department's bureaucracy. Apparently there were proper channels to be gone through...a formal application would have to be made...that application would then have to be processed...etc., etc. But this was *urgent*, he'd insisted. "I'm sure it is, I'm sure it is," the grey man on the end of the line had said, meaning: 'I'm sure it isn't, I'm sure it isn't.' "But we have many "urgent" cases to deal with, Mr Waterman, and I'm afraid we don't have a fleet of aircraft at our disposal."

Well, Dad had gone on badgering the man until at last he'd seen some sense. Because of the "special nature" of his "possible discovery", the grey man had said that they (the other grey men he worked with) would "move heaven and earth" to get an aerial photographer out to him in three or four days' time.

Yet all this had proved immaterial, for that very same day it had rained. Unexpectedly, there were showers across the south of England, and one of the places to receive a downpour was Woodcote Hill.

It had seemed almost uncanny. It had also been galling to hear people describe the rain as 'heaven-sent', 'just what was needed', 'a mercy for the gardeners', and so on - for what brought welcome relief to everyone else spelled disaster for Dad. The parched earth was watered, the grass on Woodcote Hill started growing again, and when, after several days had passed and in overcast weather the photographer flew over the Downs and took his pictures, it proved to be just as Dad had feared.

When the photos were developed, there was nothing of the chalk man to be seen.

Or, to be exact, there were one or two traces - but no-one who hadn't suspected that a chalk-cut figure had once been there would have guessed its presence from these pictures. As evidence, they just weren't sufficient.

But Dad hadn't thrown in the towel straightway. If you knew him, you'd know how diffident he was - not with me and Mum and Clara, of course, but with others - and how hard it was for him to push his point, to kick up a fuss, to set out to make a nuisance of himself. Still, he knew how important this discovery was, and he knew that he couldn't just leave it there.

So, his next step was to try to get the archaeologists involved. For awhile it looked as though some people he knew at the University were interested, but no funds were forthcoming and in the end it became all too clear that no work was actually going to be undertaken.

He also applied to the owner of the land, the National Trust. But the National Trust, South-Eastern Section, was spending the bulk of its annual budget on the refurbishment of a redundant grade II listed power station, and in any case it couldn't possibly act without more evidence.

What was he to do? What should he have done? His colleagues advised him to drop the subject, and no-one was more persistent and articulate in giving this advice than Bryan Mandeville. The gist of Dad's colleagues' advice was: "Bide your time. Don't give up, exactly, but leave it for now and bide your time. There may be another dry spell next year. Or you may find some mediaeval documents, say, that support your view that there's something carved on Woodcote Hill. But it would do more harm than good to rush the matter - it would do much more harm than good."

Academics, you see. Very conservative, very cautious.

As for Mandeville's advice, it boiled down to this: "The chances of there being something carved on that hill are approximately a million to one against. The chances of a figure from Indian mythology being carved there are infinitesimal. Therefore one concludes, old boy, that you must have had a touch of sunstroke or a serious case of wishful thinking or a drop too much sherry when you thought you saw a Shiva image there. So, unless you want to make a complete fool of yourself, you'd better forget the whole thing - and forget it now."

I guess everyone has their own internal Bryan Mandeville and, with all his diffidence, my father certainly had his. Mandeville voiced the doubts within him, and once - but only once - he came to me and said:

"You *did* see that figure on the hill, didn't you?"

"Yes."

"And you're quite sure about that?"

"Yes, absolutely."

"So, we're not crazy, then."

"No. Certainly not."

After that, he went back to the struggle. Of course, his motive was partly that he didn't want anyone else to discover the Giant before he could establish his credentials as an ancient historian, class one. It was also that, as a scholar, he saw his job as one of the revealing of knowledge, not the forgetting of knowledge. But even more than this, I think he felt that he had no choice. The vision of the dancing god had been vouchsafed to him, if you cared to put it that way, and he *had* to do something about it. He *had* to go on.

So he occupied all his available time in research. He scoured through volumes of source material in search of references to a chalk figure on the North Downs. And in six months he found just one faint clue. It was in a play by a minor Elizabethan writer, Thomas Colwell, and a friend in the English Department had put him onto it. There was a reference in Act I of the play, a rather turgid comedy called *The Merry Joiner's Journey,* to a near-legendary character who had 'vanish'd, like the chalk man of Surry'.

Notwithstanding this setback, he decided to go ahead and write a book. It would be shorter and a whole lot more personal than the dry, sober, learned account which he'd at first projected, but at least it would stamp his name upon Woodcote Hill, whatever the future brought.

He called the book *The Chalk Man Of Surrey* and planned it in five parts. In the first part, he described how he (or rather, his son) had discovered the Shiva image. In the second part, he talked of chalk figures in general and of their possible dates. In the third part, he discussed the Shiva image and its meaning: how Shiva himself personified the Spirit, the spark of God or *Atman* in Man; how here he was in his *Nataraja* form as the Lord of the Dance; how in later, more refined versions of this image (there was one in the V & A), Lord Shiva held a drum-cum-shaker in one hand and a flame in another, how his third hand was raised in a gesture of reassurance and blessing, how his fourth hand pointed at his left foot - which jutted forward outside the fiery circle of existence within which he danced, how his dance itself represented the organisation of events within the universe, and how beneath his right foot there squirmed a dwarf, signifying men who are not yet enlightened - who don't yet know their Spirit.

In the fourth part, he speculated as to when the image had been cut and by whom. Here, he asked whether this image was the only instance of an ancient figure from the Indian pantheon in the British Isles, and answered no, probably not. There was a rock in the shape of Shri Ganesha, the elephant-headed boy, the son of Lord Shiva, the symbol of innocence, on the top of Mow Cop in Cheshire. There were further Elephant Rocks on Bredon Hill and Bodmin Moor. And strangest of all, there was supposed to be an image of Shri Ganesha in a shell grotto or cave in Kent - although according to some the grotto dated only from the 18th Century and was the unrecorded work of some wealthy eccentric

In the brief closing part, Dad looked forward - rather eloquently, I thought - to his theories being proved in due course, either thanks to another drought, or through archaeological work, or both.

His intention was that the book should be copiously illustrated, not only with photographs and diagrams, but also with reproductions of the watercolours which Eric Ravilious made in the late 1930s of the Westbury White Horse, the figure of King George at Weymouth, and so on: in order to make it more attractive to the general reader as well as to his fellow academics.

But the mention of Eric Ravilious reminds me of the next thing that happened, so we'll take a break from this account of Dad's predicament and cut to the afternoon of the day on which I'd read out the Tolstoy at breakfast.

The Ravilious Bowl

One of the boarders at school had been found to have T.B., so the whole place was being fumigated. Since I had the day off, I'd joined Mum on a shopping trip to the village.

We'd been to the baker's, the greengrocer's, the butcher's and the post office, and now we were making our way back towards the car, when Mum came to a sudden halt and let out a little cry.

"Oh, look - a Ravilious plate."

"A what?"

"A Ravilious plate. Or bowl, it's a soup bowl really. That one there, do you see? It was designed by Eric Ravilious. It's part of his 'Travel' series. We used to have a whole set in the old house at Reigate, when I was your age."

We were standing outside one of the two charity shops in the village. I looked at the window display and saw the bowl at which Mum was pointing, propped between a hand-knitted tea-cosy and a large, slightly rusty tea tin. The soup bowl's central design was of a dinghy on a lake in a park. There were ornamental trees in the park and a misty sun above, and the whole was done in subtle blues and greys. I don't know why, but it made me feel calm and comfortable. I liked the designer's name as well. "*Ravilious*," I said to myself, rolling the word through my mind as though it meant 'hungry for beauty'. "*Ravilious*..."

The truth of it was that I too wanted to be a poet, though not an unpublished one. And this was another reason for Dad's depression, I suppose. He must have looked at Clara, who was studying Fine Art, or 'training to be on the dole' as it was sometimes called, and then looked at me and suspected that I too had some arty intentions (for, though I hadn't actually mentioned my poetic leanings to anyone yet, I was sometimes dangerously enthusiastic about Shakespeare, Blake and co.), and his heart must have sunk another notch within him. "Isn't there anyone in this wretched family who can take on this brutal, material world at its own game and win?" he must have wondered.

But back to the bowl in the window.

"It's got a slight chip on it," I said out loud.

"Where? Oh...so it has. But you can hardly see it, and anyway, it'll make it cheaper. It would look so nice on the dresser, and the chip's at the bottom, so it wouldn't show. I wonder how much they want for it? It might be a lot...or then again, well - let's see."

"I thought you said we couldn't afford luxuries."

"We can't. But a thing of beauty isn't a luxury, it's a necessity," Mum stated bravely, if unconvincingly.

We entered the shop, and while Mum went over to the counter to enquire about the bowl, I wandered past the musty-smelling clothes racks and the display of Oxfam's foreign goods to the bookshelf in the corner.

I needed something to read, but I wasn't sure what. A detective story, perhaps? I cast an eye over the romances, blockbusters, novels, crime books and thrillers in the paperback section.   There were a couple of Agatha Christies, but I'd read them both already. There was a well-thumbed and dog-eared edition, a late '50s Penguin, of Patrick Quentin's *The Man in the Net*, which Dad called 'the *nonpareil* of thrillers'. Or at least, that was one of the things he used to say before the black cloud had begun to settle on him...but anyway, I knew that Dad had a copy himself. I looked at the hardbacks. There were some antique copies of Dickens with tiny print, and...what was that? Tucked away on the bottom shelf between a Ford Cortina manual and a volume in German on the beauties of Frankfurt, was a book entitled **A History of the Pilgrim's Way**. It was still in its dustcover and looked unread. The price was written on a sticker on the front: only 50p.

I thought that perhaps, just perhaps, it might contain some mention of the chalk dancing man - for I knew that the Pilgrim's Way, the prehistoric chalk track which led from Wessex across the South of England and which was later associated with pilgrims to the tomb of St Thomas à Becket in Canterbury, passed close to Woodcote Hill. Of course, it was true that Dad had looked at a great many history books and found next to nothing on the subject, but I hadn't seen this book before. Maybe Dad had looked through it in London...but still, it was worth a try.

"Come on, Dan," said Mum. She had a smile on her careworn face and was holding the bowl, wrapped in second-hand tissue paper, against her chest with crossed hands.

"I'd just like to get this book, if you don't mind."

"How much is it?"

"Only 50p."

She looked at the book and paused. For a moment I thought she was thinking of the cost and was debating whether we could afford it or not, but on reflection I realised she had something else in mind. She had noted the title of the book and, having put two and two together, was wondering whether it would be a good idea - to encourage my father in his obsession. I hadn't known that she felt like this, but all at once I saw it clearly.

"All right," she said at length.

I paid and we left the shop. As we passed through the doorway I noticed, on a shelf by the window, a small metal statue of Shiva dancing calmly within his ring of fire, half-hidden behind a warped C.D. single of Ronnie Bastard's first big hit.

"Oh...look at that," I said, involuntarily.

Mum looked. "Oh dear..." she said, and the way that she said it confirmed for me the fact that she, even she, had given up the business of the Chalk Giant as a bad job, a write-off, a dud.

The Maverick

Now, to return to my father's story.

He showed his book to his colleagues and they were aghast. They didn't go for the personal touches and they didn't like the mention of the Spirit. Had he talked about a 'primitive system of belief', they might have swallowed that. Generally, they were quite happy to talk about 'primitive systems of belief', even going so far as to throw phrases like 'marvellously rich' and 'profoundly imaginative' around - but if you think they believed all that stuff, think again. And the fact that Dad had left the 'primitive belief system' bit out altogether made them blush with embarrassment. But most of all they didn't like the idea of a Shiva figure in the Stockbroker Belt. It was too outlandish by far, and they said so.

At the same time, Mandeville's sunstroke theory began to gain its adherents.

However, my father didn't listen. Or, that's to say, he listened and was badly bruised by the experience, but all the same, he'd nailed his colours to the mast, the whole department knew what he thought, and so he figured: 'I'll publish it anyway'.

Here he was in for another shock, however, for in his naivety he simply hadn't reckoned on just how difficult it is to get something into print. Of course, he'd had articles published in learned journals before now, but this was something different. The Publishing Houses didn't want books about chalk figures on hills. In particular, they didn't want books about chalk figures which probably didn't exist. Their editors must have looked at his typescript and said to themselves, "Crazy, or what?" before sending it back with the standard I'm-afraid-it's-not-quite-right-for-our-list brush-off.

Sometimes you see a boxer losing a fight. He takes any number of punches and isn't affected. Then one blow really registers, and then another, and then another, and after that it's downhill all the way. This rejection of his book by umpteen agents and publishers was the first big punch as far as Dad was concerned. The blows he'd had before - sure, they'd hurt, but this one seemed to knock the stuffing right out of him. It was the first indication he'd that, in spite of all his efforts, his dream might not become reality.

He had known all along that the learned journals weren't going to print his work, unproven as it was. But there was one other possibility: he could publish it himself.

A trip to a New Age bookshop soon cured him of that idea. He saw the sort of books with which his own would be categorised - if, at considerable expense, he did bring it out - and he had second thoughts. To a scholar, the great majority of them seemed...so thin, so airy-fairy, so infused with the Occult. And in any case, whom did they reach? Who actually *read* them?

So, he didn't publish. Instead, he would wait. He would see what happened, while continuing to lobby the archaeologists.

But then the second big blow came out of nowhere and caught him right on the chin.

He was made redundant.

It was partly that the Education cuts required that someone should be sacrificed. Now, Dad had seen this coming, but had always assumed that the first staff member to go would be Cowie, the specialist in the ancient Middle East. He was already in his sixties and was known, as a teacher, to lack that certain sparkle. Indeed, it was said that, whereas his students stayed away, insomniacs from far and wide queued up for his lectures in droves, knowing that at least they'd get some decent kip. And as for himself, Dad had assumed, unwisely, that although he wasn't yet a star in the Ancient History firmament, he was nevertheless a star-in-waiting. He had thought that this was generally understood, that only Mandeville saw it differently.

But no, Cowie was kept on and Dad lost his job. Mirchandani, the shark-suited Etruscan expert, told him privately that his work was considered unsound.

"Unsound?"

"But yes. It's thought that you're...mmm...just a little too unscientific. They wonder, with the best of intentions, if... as an academic...you've quite found your *métier*."

Dad couldn't mistake the relish with which this was said, and suddenly it seemed to him that they were all against him. Not just Mandeville, the ringleader, but Cowie and Mirchandani and Mrs Sellar, whose repertoire of Ancient Greek jokes was pronounced to be the second best in London, and even old Professor Leaman, of whom it was said that "he could think in hieroglyphics", and all the rest of them. And though you and I might imagine that, being academics, they were a bunch of bumbling eggheads, too top-heavy and absent-minded to be fast on their feet, when it came to kicking someone down the stairs of the Ivory Tower and slamming the door in his face, they were as quick as you like. From their point of view, Dad was too much the maverick. Plus, he'd been too lucky - or *almost* too lucky - and they were going to make him pay for it.

Poor old Dad. You might have wondered, from the way he now talked of his colleagues, if he was succumbing to paranoia. But it wasn't that he felt threatened by obscure, imagined forces - it was that he'd actually got the sack.

Anyway, he picked himself up off the canvas and set about getting another job. But who was interested? The Education cuts weren't just affecting London, they were slicing away at the teaching of Ancient History throughout the United Kingdom, and if there were any vacancies going, it seemed that Dad lacked the scholarly cred. As Clara liked to say, "His woolly sweaters just aren't woolly enough."

Time went by, and increasingly Dad felt himself to be a failure. Here I'm reading between the lines, of course, because he didn't come down to breakfast one morning and say, "That's it, I'm a failure," but it wasn't hard to tell that that's how he felt. Or how one part of him felt, at least. The black cloud descended upon him. You could see it weighing on his shoulders; you could see it in his eyes. He was in his mid-forties, no more, yet he must have felt that - in some respects at least - his life was all but over.

The Sculpture

That was the situation when I got back home with the book about the Pilgrim's Way. I went straight to my bedroom, which was on the ground floor at the back of the house. (Our house, which must have been designed by an amateur, had a curious lay-out. There was only one room upstairs and Clara had that, while Mum's and Dad's room was on the ground floor like mine, but on the opposite side of the house, beyond the sitting room.)

Once inside my room, I threw myself down on the bed, took out the book from the plastic carrier bag it had been put in, and opened it up.

As I did so, an enclosure slipped out and fell on the floor.

I picked it up. It seemed to be someone's letter, written on thin blue airmail paper. I let it drop to the floor again, though had there been a wastepaper bin in the room I would've probably screwed it up and thrown it in that. As it was, I fully intended to take it to the kitchen bin, once I'd leafed through the book.

I looked in the index first, under the letter 'W', then turned to the pages on Woodcote Hill. I read them all through and studied the pictures. But there was no mention of any chalk figure, either in legend or fact. Nor - so far as I could tell - was there any mention of it in the rest of the volume either. I skimmed through it briefly and put it down, dissatisfied.

More than that, I was saddened. The fact of the matter was, I suppose, that I had taken my father's quest to heart. In some way I empathized with him. The discouragement with which he had met affected me, too. The rejections that he had been accorded appeared to me to be rejections of our family as well, or at any rate, of myself. Neither he nor I had that business-minded nature which seemed so essential in these modern times. Nor did Mum, and nor - though she'd been known to raise a pencilled eyebrow at the state of inertia to which Dad's depression had brought him - did my sister.

"Oh, why can't he just *do* something," she would sometimes exclaim.

"Well, he lacks the resilience of youth, I guess," I would reply. Mind you, I was a youth myself, yet I can't say I felt particularly resilient. As a rule, poets don't.

Then she would grunt, or mutter "Ho hum", or raise another pencilled eyebrow. However, one had the peculiar feeling that in some way she was arguing with herself.

Still lying on the bed, I looked round the room. Over in front of the fireplace was a half-finished Hoptonwood stone relief of Shiva which Clara had begun about two years back. Considering her age at the time and her inexperience, it was surprisingly good. It stood about three feet high, and the dancing figure was carved with a delicate strength. She had finished and polished the face, but the hands and feet and ring of fire were only sketched in, and the dwarf had not been done at all.

She had intended it to be a present for Dad, I think, but it had taken her a long time to get as far as she had with it, and within a week of starting at Art School she had begun to lose interest in it. At Nork, apparently, the "energy level" was "just amazing" and, what with one thing and another, she'd had no time to carry on with the carving. That was the line she had taken at first. Then she'd come out with a lot of stuff about wanting "to ask questions of the spectator," and as the Shiva sculpture didn't ask any questions - or at any rate, not the ones that she wished to ask - she'd had another reason for abandoning it. And then, as time had gone on and the Chalk Giant affair had acquired a still darker, more hopeless dimension, she may have found that the sculpture had too many painful associations. Or something like that. As I think I've mentioned already, it was hard to tell what Clara really thought about anything, and it would certainly have been hard to guess, if you'd only seen her in her present, dayglo-haired, unkempt and leather-clad incarnation, that she could have carved the face of Shiva before me, with its deep and loving eyes. At any rate, the long and short of it was that she had downed tools and announced, one day last December, that she didn't really care if she never saw the thing again. I'd asked if I might have it in my room, she'd said yes - and here it was.

I looked away disconsolately and the letter on the floor - if letter it was - caught my eye. I picked it up and began to read.

The Letter

There were two unnumbered sheets. There was no address on the first and from this and the number of crossings out, I deduced that what I had in my hands was not a letter itself, but the rough draft of a letter.

It was the first words, however, that really caught my eye.

"My dear Bryan," it said.

"Well, what's so striking in that?" you ask. The answer is the 'y' in Bryan. Mostly, Brian is spelled with an 'i'. The fancier version is rarer, and I only knew of one man who spelled his name that way.

Dad's enemy, Bryan Mandeville.

Of course, it was probably a coincidence - it was almost certainly a coincidence - but all the same, I read on. And this is what I read:

My dear Bryan,

I must thank you for the Belgian truffles - a most unexpected gift, and one entirely to my taste! I confess I have eaten them all already, leaving none for you should you wish to call again.

And I think I may safely say that, once you have heard my news, you will wish to call again. Something has occurred - something which, for various reasons, I would rather not discuss on the 'phone.

But what is my news? you are asking yourself. What is it that has occurred? It is simply this: <u>I have been reading Bastable</u>.

But what is 'Bastable'? you inquire again.

Well, you will forgive me, I am sure, my dear Bryan, if at this early stage I do not become too <u>specific</u>. I will say this much, though: it is a manuscript from the late Seventeenth Century, and almost certainly it is the only one in existence. I purchased it years ago, shortly after the War, when such items were still to be had, as they say, 'for a song' - but I have never had occasion to read it until now.

Indeed, I do not know why it came into my mind to read it. But it is fortunate that I did, for within its somewhat timeworn pages Mr Bastable mentions something very, very interesting <u>re</u> you know what.

I really feel we must have another little <u>tête à tête</u> and...what's the phrase? <u>Talk terms</u>.

But I must tell you one other thing. There have been a few burglaries in this area of late and I have had to take measures to secrete certain valuables where even the most assiduous thief cannot find them. Among those valuables I have seen fit to place my Bastable.

I merely mention this in passing, and for no other reason. Though I must admit that a man who has found out my weakness for chocolate truffles is a man to be reckoned with

And there, in mid-flight, the draft broke off.

I put the letter down, my head spinning. In the time it had taken me to read those two sheets of paper, everything had become transformed!

Or had it? Had anything really changed, or was I being absurdly over-optimistic?

I told myself to calm down and look coolly at the facts. And the first and most outstanding fact, from my point of view, was a phrase which didn't appear in the letter as I have recorded it, but which was in one of the sentences that had been crossed out. As far as I could tell - for it needed some deciphering - the writer's first version of "something very, very interesting <u>re</u> you know what" had been "something very, very interesting <u>re</u> the chalk figure".

Which clinched it, as far as I was concerned. It confirmed the intuition I'd had that the addressee was Bryan Mandeville, and it proved that the subject was none other than our own Chalk Giant.

But what else did it tell us? I tried to make some deductions.

Firstly, the obvious things. The writer had a manuscript which, he had good reason to believe, contained some important information about the Shiva figure. This manuscript was unique - therefore no-one but the letter-writer could have access to this information.

Secondly, the writer didn't trust Mandeville much. He was letting him know that he'd hidden the manuscript, not just in order to be chatty, but because he wanted Mandeville to be aware that he couldn't just walk in and grab it, should that be his idea.

Whether the writer had a reason to be cautious, or whether it was merely that he had a suspicious and secretive nature, was hard to tell. There was something about his fussy, pedantic, old-womanish style which suggested that the latter explanation might be the right one... And yet, from what little I knew of Mandeville, he was scarcely a man to be trusted. It wasn't just that the way he'd treated Dad spoke of a harsh, ungenerous character; it was that there seemed something...well, almost *unbalanced* about the way he'd opposed Dad's ideas.

I'd met him three times. The first had been at home, in the heady days soon after Dad's appointment as a lecturer. Dad had invited two or three of his new academic pals round to dinner, and Bryan Mandeville had been one of them. Since his and Dad's main interests in the Ancient History field overlapped, and since he lived in our part of the world, you might have thought that they would have got on well. They didn't.

I don't think it was Dad's fault. Mandeville turned out to be a short, tough, brainy-looking man with a receding hairline and little tufts of hair which sprouted out from his collar, as though he were wearing thermal underwear made from gorilla hide. He also had an air of being about to lose his temper and, considering that he'd been invited to dinner, his manner was hardly what you'd call gracious.

The fact that Dad's special subject was Ancient British History seemed, if anything, to make him feel threatened. Maybe it was just that he too was worried about his job security. And then, the *comfortableness* of Dad's domestic life (for things at home were comfortable, back then) seemed to make him resentful - for although he had a family, he and his wife had separated. Hence, he slipped into one of those bristling, clever, competitive moods to which intellectuals are prone, and made everyone feel uneasy.

That, at least, was my analysis.

As for my third encounter with Bryan Mandeville, it had been when Dad had cut him dead that day in Epsom.

But, as I now realised, it was the second occasion on which I'd seen him that provided the most food for thought.

It had happened one afternoon around the time that Dad had been canvassing his colleagues' support for his book. I'd been out for a stroll by myself to Woodcote Hill. You have to go up a private road to get there, and only the people who live there are supposed to use their cars; the plebs have to park elsewhere and walk. On this particular evening, however, I noticed a car on the verge near where the footpath led off to the Hill. That in itself struck me as unusual - then I saw who its probable owner was. I'd taken the footpath and had just reached the part where you go through thick woods before emerging on the hilltop, when who should be coming towards me, binoculars round his thick, stumpy neck and an I-know-something-you-don't expression on his face, but Bryan Mandeville.

I hadn't been going to say anything, not only because I'd had nothing to say, but also because the animus he bore my father had come out into the open by then and he could hardly have expected me to be friendly.

Rather to my surprise, however, he stopped and spoke to me.

"Ah...now let me see. It's Ned Waterman's son, isn't it?"

"Yes," I said, much taken aback. He'd exchanged the I-know-something-you-don't expression for an I'm-always-glad-to-pass-the-time-of-day-with-the-younger-generation one, though something of the former was still showing through the cracks in the latter, if you follow me.

"I'm afraid I forget your name..."

"Dan."

"Of course. Daniel. Hebrew: *God has judged* - "

"Actually, it's short for Dante."

That's a secret I don't often let out and, as I had anticipated, it stopped him in his tracks. He didn't follow it up - he didn't even come out with some quip about meeting me in a dark wood - he merely said, rather hurriedly, I thought, "Well, Dan, you've caught me indulging my hobby." He tapped his binoculars. "Bird watching. There's said to be a hoopoe about - the first for thirty-five years - though I can't say I've had the good fortune to see it."

"A hoopoe?"

"Yes. You know your *Conference of the Birds*, I dare say. Well, don't let me keep you. My regards to your father..."

And with that he'd marched off to his car.

Strange? Undeniably - and I'd thought so at the time. The bird watching bit had seemed scarcely credible, and the fact that he'd actually stopped to talk to me and to explain away the binoculars had served only to underline how mysterious his behaviour was. If he'd been looking for hoopoes, I was a Dutchman.

Of course, I'd assumed that in reality he'd been doing research. He'd been checking that his belief was right - that the Chalk Giant did not exist. Say what you like about him, but he was after all a scholar and would have wanted to be sure of his ground before denouncing Dad.

But the letter in front of me suggested a different explanation. He hadn't been trying to *disprove* the Chalk Giant's existence, he had been trying *to see it for himself!* From the first he must have sensed - or feared - that Dad was on to something genuine, and therefore he was doing all he could to deter Dad from publishing - in order that he could pip him to the post and claim the find for himself!

This theory made his behaviour that day much more intelligible. If he'd been making sure to his own satisfaction that the chalk figure was just an illusion of Dad's - which we already knew that he thought (or pretended to think) - then why should he have gone to all that trouble to make me believe he was bird-watching? He could have just said, "Hello Sonny. I've been looking for non-existent Chalk Giants, the Indian variety - pah!" and laughed a thin, derisive laugh. But if he'd actually been hunting for traces of the Shiva figure, then it wasn't so surprising that he should have tried to cover his tracks. He'd wanted me to think that he had no interest in the figure, when really he was desperate to find it.

Now...what more could I deduce from this letter?

That the writer was old. There was something old-fashioned about the apostrophe before 'phone' - but in any case he referred to having bought the manuscript just after the War. If he'd been around twenty-five in 1945, then he would be around 75 now.

I say 'he' because the handwriting seemed to be that of a man's. Still, I supposed that the writer could have been a woman.

But as to where he (or she) lived, and who he (or she) was, I was completely in the dark - as Clara was quick to point out when, a little later, I mentioned it to her.

Clara's Doubts

I didn't go straight to Dad with the letter, as you might have imagined, because I didn't want to raise his hopes when I had so little to go on. Indeed, I didn't really want to raise the subject with him at all - so painful had it become for him, for me, for all of us.

Likewise, I didn't want to go to Mum - yet. But I had to tell someone about it and, besides, I needed someone to consult. For all of twenty seconds I toyed with the notion of ringing a school friend. But the fact that none of them lived within walking distance, and the thought of all the effort involved in having to drag their attention away from MTV or from their skateboarding practice in order to listen to my story dissuaded me. Besides, I wanted to keep the business within the family. So I went to Clara.

She'd got back early from Nork and was sorting out dirty laundry in her room. I told her the story and showed her the letter. Making no comment and not altering her blank expression, unless to make it blanker, she took the two sheets of paper and read them.

"Well..?" I asked excitedly, once she'd come to the end and had handed them back.

"Well what?"

"Well - doesn't it grab you? Can't you see how important this is?"

45

Maddeningly, she didn't answer at first. Then she said, "Not really, no."

"But the 'Bryan' must be Mandeville, right?"

"Not 'must'. Though I suppose it *might* be, yes..."

"And the whole thing's about the Chalk Giant..."

"Well, yes, I suppose so."

"And what the writer's saying, in as many words, is that he's got some proof that it really does exist."

Clara put down the dirty socks she was holding and put on her most elder-sisterly voice. "Look, Dan, he *may* have some proof, or he may be completely gaga. You just don't know. You don't know who he is." She spelled this out slowly, as if I were still in Primary School. "He could be anyone. You don't know where he lives. He could live on the other side of the Moon, Dan. He could live on the far side of the Moon and be as crazy as a squirrel."

"I didn't know squirrels were crazy," I said huffily.

"And look - who knows when he wrote the letter? Or whether he sent a copy to Mandeville? I mean, this could be ancient history, Dan. Mandeville, if Mandeville's the man, could've gone and seen him with a whole *sack* load of truffles and sorted it all out long ago."

"Well, maybe... But if so, how come we haven't heard anything? If my theory's correct and Mandeville's been itching to prove that the Shiva image really does exist, he's not going to have hung about, is he?" I argued.

But Clara wasn't convinced. "Oh, this is all just *speculation*," she said airily. "It's too much for me." She picked up the socks again and grabbed a paint-stained crop top for good measure.

"Oh, but Clara, can't you *see*?" I countered. "I mean, where's your *imagination*?"

That got to her all right.

"Here. Right here," she said tapping her bright red hair. I presumed she was referring to the brain beneath. "But if you really want to know, I think you're simply *deluding* yourself if you believe this letter's going to help. And anyway, who's 'Bastable'? What's 'Bastable'?" she went on in a bored, know-nothing voice.

Do you ever watch American sitcoms? She sounded like she had a guest part on one. The English girl, a little kooky.

"Bastable's the key to it all. If we could get our hands on Bastable, we'd have the proof we need."

"Oh? Well, just how do you propose to get your hands on something when you don't know where it is - *and* when it's in a secret hiding place, anyway?"

She had a point, of course. I didn't know. I didn't have a clue. Yet I felt sure that somehow there must be a way.

"And another thing, Dan. This Bastable's a Seventeenth Century thing. But that's surely too late for Dad's purposes. I mean, if the Chalk Giant was visible in the 1650s, say, and this manuscript says it was, then why wasn't Dad able to find more material about it?"

This one was also hard to answer. To tell you the truth, it hadn't even occurred to me that it might be a problem. Historically speaking, though, the Seventeenth Century was fairly recent - and Clara was therefore right. If there was a record of the Giant in the Seventeenth Century, how come it wasn't better known? How come there weren't other records, or even maps, with the Chalk Giant mentioned?

In addition to this, there was the revelation of just how jaded Clara had become. I suppose I'd hoped that at the very least she would have adopted a neutral attitude towards the letter, yet she'd been negative from the first. Indeed, the only time she had shown any signs of interest had been just now, when she'd made the point about Bastable being too modern.

But if even Clara was against going on, that left only me to fight the good fight on Dad's behalf, and I didn't know if I was up to it.

I was about to continue to try to bring her round, therefore, when - revealingly twisting the laundry in her hands - she took up the theme again herself.

"Actually this is all pretty academic," she said.

"'Pretty academic'? What do you mean?"

"Your pursuit of some shred of evidence to support Dad's theory. It's all neither here nor there."

I took a step back, preparing myself for a shock.

Clara's Bombshell

"Oh, why's that?" I asked.

"Because pretty soon the whole hill's going to be dug up."

"'Dug up'? What do you mean, 'dug up'? Have they discovered oil, or something?"

Clara gave up twisting the laundry and dropped it on the floor again. "It's like this," she said. "Sohrab's had this amazing idea."

"Oh yeah? Try it out on me," I responded, and if I sounded a mite aggressive, not to mention sceptical, it was because I'd heard of this Sohrab before. But more of that in a moment.

"He's-going-to-carve-a-new-chalk-figure-on-the-hill," she said all in a rush. "It's a big project. It's pretty mega, actually. He's got the backing of English Heritage and the Lottery Fund *and* the Millennium Commission. It's all to do with the Millennium celebrations. It's to be done in time for that."

Inwardly, I reeled. Outwardly, I tried to stay calm. "When you say 'the hill', you mean - "

"Woodcote Hill, yes."

"And when did he get this brilliant idea?"

"Oh, some time ago. You can't get big artistic projects like this together overnight, you know."

"And what sort of picture is he going to carve?"

She replied readily enough, though not to my question. "Well, I don't know that *he's* going to carve it. He's going to be more a sort of overseer, if you know what I mean."

"Yeah, I think I know what you mean. You mean, Sohrab's not actually going to get his trowel out and start scraping away; he's going to leave that to people like you, while he sits in his deckchair and says, 'A bit more to the right, no, hold it, a bit more to the left. Oh, and make the next martini a little drier, will you?' But you still haven't answered the question. What's the figure going to be?"

There was a slight pause, as though Clara was standing on a high diving board, wondering whether she was going to fit into, or even hit, the bucket of water far, far away beneath her.

"Ronnie Bastard," she said at last.

This time I reeled outwardly as well. "You can't be serious!"

"He's a very important artist - "

"Like Sohrab Quine, I suppose - "

"And, more to the point, he's a flag-waver for Britpop."

"He's a what for what?"

"A flag-waver for Britpop. *You* know. And that's why the Millennium Commission's got behind the project. Sohrab put forward a lot of ideas, I can tell you - his mind's just so... so *fertile* - but this is the one that they really liked. They feel that an image of Ronnie is just what's needed to celebrate Britain in the year 2000."

"'*Celebrate*'?" I said. "Are you sure the word was 'celebrate'?"

She ignored me. "Oh, I know what you're thinking. You're thinking he's too contemporary, and if they're going to carve something in the chalk it should be, I don't know, a Morris dancer or St George or a thatched cottage, something *old* and *quaint*. But the Commissioners want something up to date. That's the whole point. They're not *retrophiliacs*. They don't want something *prehistoric*," said Clara, pronouncing 'old' and 'quaint' as though they were terms of the severest reprobation.

Okay, I thought, okay, fair enough, why not? But...*Ronnie Bastard*?

I suppose that everyone's heard the story of Ronnie Bastard and *The Bastards* more times than they've had hot dinners, but I'll run through it once more anyway. First, the name. Unlikely though it may seem, 'Bastard' was once a normal, acceptable surname, if not a common one. Take, for instance, the Bastards, John and William, who rebuilt the pleasant Dorset town of Blandford Forum after the devastating fire of 1731. Maybe Ronnie Bastard and his hell-raising brother Tycho 'The Psycho' Bastard were descendants of theirs - though it's more likely that, being performers, they simply adopted the name. Anyway, what matters is that they formed a rock band, *The Bastards*, and made it big. Or rather, not big but *huge*, gigantic, mega-colossal. Some time after conquering America, however, the brothers had a falling out and Tycho quit to form a new wave country and western outfit, *The Snake-Eyed Bastards*. Furious that Tycho was keeping a part of the band's name, Ronnie sued him for 'theft of intellectual property'. When the resulting court case threatened to ruin them both, they patched up their differences and, together with their cousin Calvin, formed a new and even more globally successful band, *The Complete Bastards*. (True, purists objected to Calvin's inclusion in the group, pointing out that he was only a cousin by marriage - but whenever quizzed on this point, insiders always said he was 'a real Bastard' too.) When they cleaned up at the Grammys, Ronnie more or less summed things up by announcing: "It's official – we're bigger than God." And if at the time of which I'm writing you were under thirty and you didn't own at least something by 'The Completes', as their many fans called them - well, you were in a small minority, let me tell you.

All the same, whether ageing bad boy Ronnie, the master of the two-chord punk anthem, merited having so much as a stale jelly doughnut modelled after him was another matter.

Meanwhile, I didn't know what to say. I paused, and the silence was a vacuum demanding to be filled. I said: "Well, personally I thought Ronnie Bastard was last year's thing. By the year 2000 he'll be as dead as the Charleston. And, anyway, what do you think Dad's going to say?"

At Dinner

We found out at dinner. I spent most of it musing on the subject of Sohrab Quine, whom I had never met, but whom I knew to have long been an important figure in Clara's pantheon.

He was a post-graduate student who also did some lecturing at her college, and during her early days there we had regularly been treated to rapturous descriptions of his amazing teaching methods, brilliant ideas, and inspirational personality. It was Quine who had 'deconstructed' Clara's outdated conditioning, taught her the importance of using materials correctly, shown her that Michelangelo, Canova and co., had they been around today, would have been knocking out exactly the sort of things that, well, Sohrab Quine was knocking out, and placed before her the kind of artists who made large metal cubes covered in iron filings or huge polystyrene hamburgers - and, of course, himself - as the models to be emulated. I hadn't actually seen his work, but as far as I was concerned, when you'd heard that for his degree show he had exhibited an empty room, albeit one that was 'subtly modified', you'd heard all there was to hear about it.

As a matter of fact, although I hadn't actually seen Sohrab or his work, I *had* been to Clara's college once - and on a trip to the men's room there I'd read the graffiti inscribed on the toilet roll dispenser. "Arts Degrees. Please take one," some wag had written, and when you looked at the case of Sohrab Quine, you could see what he'd meant.

Anyway, Clara was looking paler and eating even less than usual, which prompted Mum to ask her what the matter was. I kicked her under the table, as though to say: "Get on with it, then," and, reluctantly yet hurriedly, she did get on with it. She told Dad all, and her explanation went like this:

"Dad, there's going to be a figure carved on Woodcote Hill. It's to do with the Millennium Commission and English Heritage and all that."

It seemed to take awhile for this to make an impression on Dad. At length, though, he poked forth his head from his shell and said, "What?"

In a dry, brittle voice, Clara repeated her statement.

Dad looked aghast. In fact, he looked stricken, and I could have sworn that his face turned grey.

"What are you talking about?" he managed.

"What I said. It's a fact, Dad."

"Clara, is this true?" asked Mum. She sounded sincerely concerned - for as she must have known, if it *was* true, it spelled the end of all Dad's dreams.

"It's a fact," Clara said again. Her voice seemed to come from a long way off.

"But...but how do you know about this?" Dad asked.

"Well, it's the talk of the College, for one thing - "

"It doesn't have anything to do *with* the College, does it?" he retorted sharply.

This question must have made Clara uncomfortable, for she withdrew still further into the cool, hard demeanour at which she'd worked so assiduously for the last half-year.

"I guess so," she said, almost shrugging. "It was Sohrab's idea. Actually, it's going to be amazing. It'll be one of the biggest works of art of modern times. It's to celebrate the Millennium."

Then Dad asked what the figure was to be of, and Clara told him, and there was what I suppose you would call a deathly hush.

"But I guess you may not have heard of him," added Clara.

"Of course I've heard of him! More to the point, I've *heard* him! How can I not hear him when you play his 'music' so damned loud! *Material Boy*, *You Turn Me Off*, and what's that new one - *Everything Sucks* - oh yes, oh yes, I've *heard* him," exploded Dad.

Once or twice before in this account I've likened him to a boxer. Well, now he must have felt like a boxer who, having been battered and biffed for all of ten rounds and at last knocked out, therefore losing his title, was now being mugged in the car park.

Then he seemed to think of something. Something which, incidentally, I hadn't thought to ask myself.

"But what I don't understand is how Quine came to pick *Woodcote* Hill. There are enough hills to choose from around here, I would have thought. It just seems a strange coincidence that he should have chosen Woodcote

Hill..." He said this sadly, as if there was no answering the question, no comprehending the ways of Fate.

Then a further thought - the obvious one - must have assailed him, for, turning from grey to red - an angry, shadowy red - he addressed Clara thus:

"It wasn't *you* who suggested Woodcote Hill, was it?"

Clara did shrug this time. Her voice sounded more brittle than ever. "I didn't *suggest* it, no. It was all his idea. And apparently, Woodcote Hill is the best hill for the purpose. He had a, you know, a *feasibility study* done. But, well, yes, I guess I did just maybe mention your Shiva idea to him."

In a flash I saw what I hadn't seen before: that Clara - my sister Clara - cool, black-clad, cold-voiced, hardboiled, modern-girl Clara - carried some sort of torch, or at least a lit match, for Sohrab Quine. It was probably the sort of thing you would expect a new girl to have for the College's star and I doubted that it had been reciprocated. Indeed, until this present affair we hadn't heard quite so much about friend Sohrab of late - but all the same, there it was. Pretty soon after starting at Nork, Clara must have opted for a hero-worship course in *Quine, S.* And in her eagerness to impress her new idol-cum-guru, the Bernini of Nork, she must have told him of Dad's idea about the Chalk Giant on Woodcote Hill.

And then a light bulb had gone on above his head and he'd exclaimed, "Hey, that gives *me* an idea! I could do something like that myself! Yeah...a chalk figure...something vast and controversial, with loads of shock value...why, it should even get on the national News. And as for money, we could get those Millennium dudes to back it. Hey, yeah, wow, how do I think of these things?" etc, etc.

I suppose that Dad, who, although depressed, was no slouch intellectually, must have seen the same sort of picture - for he now turned from red to white: the white of someone who's about to be sick. "And this...this project is definitely going ahead, you say?"

"Uh-huh, definitely. It should be starting in about a fortnight, I think. They just need to get the National Trust to okay it. They're the landowners, of course, and they've got some big meeting about it in two weeks' time. But there shouldn't be any problem. Sohrab says it's in the bag."

The Young Detective

I woke in the middle of the night. So deeply had I been asleep that it took me a moment or two to remember the terrible thing had happened. Or the two terrible things, I should say, for as well as the fact that a giant-sized image of Ronnie Bastard was going to be carved on Woodcote Hill, there was also the little matter of Clara's betrayal.

At least, if she hadn't exactly betrayed Dad in telling Quine about the Shiva figure, it was inadvertently thanks to her that he'd become 'inspired'. It was Clara who'd, as it were, switched on that light bulb above his head. And having done so, she was siding with him and his project, not with Dad.

The subject had been revived after dinner, though not with Clara present. She'd gone upstairs to her room to console herself, or steel herself, with a repeated playing of Ronnie's latest hit. Strains of *'Everything s-s-s-s-s-s-sucks'* complete with mind-numbing backbeat had oozed down into the dining room.

Mum had said some comforting words but Dad had been too shocked to respond to them. He'd simply sat there with a blank look on his face and his arms hanging limp at his sides, like a gingerbread man that's just had its legs bitten off. Then he'd suddenly come alive in a rather worrying, exaggerated way, as though someone had plugged him into the mains. Words had tumbled indistinctly out of his mouth, mostly to the effect that at least he and Ronnie had one thing in common - they didn't think much of things.

Then, calming down a little, he'd dwelt at length on the irony of how those from whom, in his dream unveiling Lord Shiva on Woodcote Hill, he might have expected the most support - the scholars and artists - had turned out to be just the ones who were being most obstructive.

After this, I had gone to bed.

I still hadn't mentioned the letter, but as far as I was concerned, it afforded the one chink of light in the whole gloomy affair. What I'd got to do now, I determined, after mulling it over in bed, was to go to the Charity Shop again and find out, if I could, where the book on the Pilgrim's Way had come from. I'd have to play the part of the young detective: there was no other choice.

I was all too well aware how long a shot it would be. I'd sometimes seen people come into charity shops with boxes of books or clothes, dump them by the counter, and swiftly return to their cars before somebody nicked them or they got a parking ticket, without much more than a "Here you are, then," and a cheery wave. To the people who worked in the shops, these donors were as good as anonymous - and besides, the goods they brought in might not have been their own. They might have belonged to some relative, recently deceased, or to a neighbour, or to the people they'd bought their house from, etc.

And even if the donor of the Pilgrim's Way book had been known to the person behind the counter, the latter might not now - some time later - be able to connect the two.

These dispiriting thoughts occurred to me as I entered the Oxfam Shop the next morning. It was a Friday, but I was still off school because of the fumigation. I wouldn't be going back until Monday.

A florid, late-middle-aged woman was serving. I showed her the book and asked, a little hesitantly, if she could remember who'd brought it in.

"Oh, no, dear. We get so many books."

"It probably came in quite recently. I bought it yesterday, and I shouldn't think it had been in here for long." I based this deduction on the book's quality. Obscure, tatty books sometimes stayed on Oxfam Shop shelves for ages, but good quality books, if not absurdly overpriced, were usually snapped up within a day or two.

She looked at the book again.

"I can't say it rings any bells, dear. But then, I've only just started working here, you see."

"Well, who might have been here when the book was brought in? If it was during the last week, I mean."

"Oh, now you're asking. It could have been anyone."

A few seconds ticked by. I wasn't sure whether she was thinking of possible people, or whether she had just switched off.

"Well, could you give me a name?"

"James, John, Jack, Peter, Charles - how many do you want?" she answered, and cackled uproariously. Then, as if a button had been pressed, she sobered up. "Well, there *is*

61

Fred. He's usually in here on Mondays and Tuesdays," she said. Then she added in a stage whisper: "Trouble is, he's a bit simple. Oh, but I know," she went on, reverting to her normal voice, "There's Dorothy. Dorothy's the person you want to ask. If anybody would remember, it's Dorothy."

I sighed with relief. "And how do I get in touch with her?"

The woman's mouth twitched and she threatened to cackle again. I wondered whether her hair, which was gingery and abundant, was in fact a wig. "You don't," she said bluntly. "She's in Tunisia on her holidays. Went over with her son and his family. I don't think she'll be back for a fortnight, at least."

I sighed again, though this time without relief. The young detective was having no luck. Meanwhile, another customer came up to the counter and the woman turned to him. I began to walk towards the door, feeling that our only hope was if the National Trust's decision on Quine's idea should be delayed.

Then, when I was half-way out of the door, I suddenly had a thought.

People didn't usually donate just *one* book to a shop like this; they donated several at a time. So, what if there should be other books here left by the man who'd written the letter, and what if one of them had his name in it? It was often the case that people wrote their names in their books, and the writer of the letter had struck me as just the type to do so.

I hurried across to the shelves and, to the puzzlement of a young woman standing beside me, started looking at the flyleaves of the books. I avoided the *Mills and Boon* romances and the children's books, but raced through the rest. And some did indeed have their late owners' names in them - but not in the handwriting used in the letter. After two shelves, I paused. Was there any book there which would square with the image I had formed of a fussy pedant?

There was. *From A To Z Including Y: A Lexicographer's Notes* caught my eye. I turned the cover and saw a label inside. It read: *Ex Libris: James Aitken-Sneath.* The name seemed to fit the bill, but unfortunately it was printed and therefore proved nothing.

Then I noticed a copy of Cobbett's *Rural Rides*. Cobbett, I had read somewhere, had been particularly fond of the view from Woodcote Hill and had ridden there often. This tied in loosely with the theme of the volume in my hand - the volume on the Pilgrim's Way - and it struck me that the same man might have owned them both.

He had.

On the flyleaf was written in ink the legend: *James Aitken-Sneath, Smithers' Bookshop, Guildford, 1953* - and the handwriting, though firmer, was essentially the same as that of the man who had written the letter to Mandeville.

I put the book back in the shelf with a smile. I had reached my first goal.

A Blue Funk

Now, what next? Was I to visit Mr Aitken-Sneath and ask him to show me the Bastable? Was I to pose - or, better, ask Clara to pose (for surely I looked too young) as a student who'd got wind of the fact that he owned an original Bastable and would give her right arm to see it? Or should I pretend to be Bastable's descendant? Or...

The trouble with all these alternatives was that I had no idea whom Bastable had been. Still, the first thing I had to do was to find out where Aitken-Sneath lived. I was confident that it must be nearby, else why should his books have been donated here?

Yet when I looked in the phone book, he wasn't listed. I was disappointed, of course, but not really surprised. True, it might have meant that he didn't live in our area at all...but I didn't think it *proved* that. I'd had a feeling all along that someone with the personality revealed in the letter would be ex-directory.

Okay - the next most likely place to enquire, I considered, was in the village newsagent's. An elderly, cultured man like Aitken-Sneath would no doubt have a newspaper delivered, and therefore the newsagent would know his address.

The shop was further back along the high street, near the Victorian red-brick church, and it took me no more than a couple of minutes to reach it and ask my question of the affable Mr Cuff, the manager.

"Oh yes, I know Mr Aitken-Sneath," he answered straightway, and my spirits soared. "...The old antiquarian chap. Now, let me see," he went on, closing his eyes in an effort of memory, "Takes the *Daily Telegraph*, *Sunday Telegraph*, *Country Life*, *The Field* and *The Surrey Gazette*. Always pays on the nail."

Then his manner changed, he adopted the expression of a man at his Sunday prayers and his voice took on a quieter, more sepulchral note. "Or did, that is. He died - oh, three, four weeks ago. But you knew that, I suppose?"

"Well, no. No, I didn't," I managed, my spirits plummeting.

"Oh, yes. Died three or four weeks ago. Ah, we lost a good customer there. Always paid on the nail - on the nail. Very sad, very sad. A heart attack, they said. He'd had a dicky ticker for a long time."

"And he lived near here?" I suggested.

"Up at *The Junipers*. Up your way, in fact. Do you know it? By Woodcote Hill."

I said yes, I did know it, thanked him, eluded his question as to why I'd asked about Mr Aitken-Sneath by pretending deafness, and left the shop. Then, hardly knowing what I was doing, I set off for home. It was a good three mile walk, and I'd only just come into the village - but that didn't matter. I needed time to think things over.

And the first item on the agenda was this fact of Aitken-Sneath's demise. It put a different, much more complex complexion on things.

Yet maybe it wasn't as disastrous as I'd at first supposed. For one thing, it meant that I wouldn't have to face Aitken-Sneath himself. If he'd been as suspicious of others' motives as his letter suggested, then I would have had a hard job on my hands, trying to get to see his manuscript.

Secondly, it might explain why things had been so quiet on the Mandeville front. It seemed likely that either Aitken-Sneath had died before sending the finished version of his letter, or else he *had* sent the letter, yet had died before 'talking terms' - which meant that Mandeville hadn't yet seen the proof of the Chalk Giant's existence which, purportedly, the Bastable book contained. In either case, he would be as much in the dark as I was. And all this time, the Bastable manuscript was still lying somewhere in a hiding place at *The Junipers*, Woodcote Hill.

Needless to say, the fact of Aitken-Sneath's death also explained just what his books - or three of them, at least - were doing in the Oxfam Shop. And, finally, the mention of *The Junipers* and 'the old antiquarian' was rekindling a memory. *The Junipers*, I knew, was a house set back from the brow of Woodcote Hill behind a high brick wall. The grounds extended some distance through the woods along the hilltop to a point where the wall gave way to a barbed-wire fence. A few years back, the owner - now revealed as Aitken-Sneath - had fixed a number of signs to this fence. Not your usual unfriendly KEEP OUT signs either, mind you, but downright nasty KEEP OUT signs. Guard dogs patrolled these grounds, the passer-by was told in no uncertain manner - and in case he couldn't read, a picture showed a savage sort of bulldog biting someone's leg. Not nice. The path to Woodcote Hill ran next to this fence and both Mum and Dad had taken exception to these signs when they'd first appeared, while Clara had been liberal in her use of the terms 'fascist' and 'ghetto mentality'. She'd also cast doubt on the whole notion of private property, and one could see her point. These signs, the barbed wire, and the broken glass which the owner had had embedded in cement on the top of the high brick wall not only had a depressing effect and spoiled the charm of the walk, but the fact that neither Mum nor Dad nor Clara nor I had ever seen anyone *in* the private woods beyond the fence made one wonder if the fence itself was really that necessary. The woods, in their undisturbed, dark quietness always looked mysterious and inviting, and one fine day, Clara and I had often told each other, we would jolly well break into them and see for ourselves what these famous guard dogs were really like - for of course we hadn't believed that they existed. We had never actually got round to going in, however.

Now, we'd known that some sort of 'antiquarian', well-versed in local history, lived there - and for awhile Dad had considered approaching him for information about the history of Woodcote Hill. Indeed, I think he'd once set off to go and see him - but the barred gates and the broken glass and the thought of the guard dog signs had put him off.

Besides, he'd reasoned that if this antiquarian had known anything about the chalk giant, he would long since have made his knowledge public.

But Mandeville hadn't been half so sensitive. He too must have heard of this local historian and had gone to consult him. Then Aitken-Sneath had started reading Bastable. And then he'd died.

That was the gist of my thoughts, and by the time I'd thought them all, I'd reached the white gate beyond which lay our cul-de-sac. The latter led off to the right, but if you took the longer, left-hand lane instead, you'd eventually come to *The Junipers*. I decided to go there straightaway on the principle that there was no time like the present for doing what you had to do. But after half a dozen steps I changed my mind. I still hadn't worked out a story - and there might not be anyone in - and I needed a drink - and all in all it could wait till the afternoon. In other words, I was in a blue funk.

Sohrab Quine

I made up my mind that, come what may, I would visit *The Junipers* after lunch - though quite what I was going to do when I got there, I wasn't sure. Lunch came and went, however, and likewise the siesta hour - and likewise a further hour - before I felt I really couldn't put it off any longer.

But I did, for just then we had a visitor.

It was none other than Sohrab Quine. He arrived in a battered white convertible - an ancient Hillman Imp - with Clara, a blonde, and a sidekick in tow. They'd come from their college in order to examine the site of Quine's proposed Chalk Giant: to 'work out the logistics' of how many metres of tape would be needed to mark out the shape, how many stakes would be needed to keep the tape in place, how many volunteers would be needed to remove the surface soil, how many shovels they'd need, and so on. And since they were passing, they'd thought they might drop in for a cup of tea, explained Clara to Mum. "Or iced lager," the sidekick amended.

The sidekick's name was Jez; the blonde's, if I heard aright, was Fliss. Clara made the introductions in a way that was at one and the same time sullen, as though she felt a trifle guilty for bringing Dad's Nemesis here, and bold, as though she were daring - just daring - Mum or me to kick up a fuss. In fact, the combination of two such different moods made me think of an angry sheep. Especially when she came to introduce Quine.

"And this is Sohrab," she bleated, eyes blazing, as Quine issued lazily forth from the car. I had long been curious to see what Quine looked like, and now I knew. The first thing that struck you about him was his size. He was tall and broad, with long thick hair and an almost-handsome face which was all the uglier for being not-quite-handsome, if you know what I mean. It was as if there'd been a last minute change of plan on the production line when they'd manufactured him. The foreman must have supposed that Quine was meant to be good-looking in a chunky, square-jawed way, when some sharp-eyed factory hand, noticing the label 'Smart-ass' on the product, had at the last minute readjusted the lathe. The result was a face that was just *too* chunky, and a jaw that, while square enough, was also slightly out of kilter, giving him a sort of smug-but-brutish look.

Not that Sohrab himself seemed upset by this. Perhaps he didn't look in mirrors, which I doubted, or perhaps no-one had got round to telling him, "Look, Sohrab, for the good of the community, could you wear a paper bag over your head? We'll punch some eyeholes in it, of course, and there'll be an extra hole so you can eat, but, really, you know...the public must be protected!" At any rate, it was easy to see how he viewed himself. He had 'Cool Dude' written all over him. Quite literally. It was on his T-shirt. *COOL* was on the front in big red letters a foot and a half high, in case you were short-sighted, and *DUDE* was on the back, ditto.

"You must be Clara's Mum," he said as he ambled across the forecourt. He stretched out a huge hand and added, "Hi, Clara's Mum."

I took a step to the side in case he should punch me on the shoulder with a "Hi, Kid, how're y'doing?", but he didn't. He merely ignored me.

Transparently ill-at-ease, Mum asked them in. They filed into the sitting room - a long, cosy room with windows at either end - while she went off to make the tea. I went with her, thinking to take refuge from our guests - but was surprised to find that as soon as the tea was in the pot, Mum hastened back into the sitting room.

My first thought was that she must be worried in case Quine should take it into his head to start 'subtly modifying' our house while her back was turned. Then I saw the obvious. She was concerned about Dad. She was worried that he might enter from the garden unawares - when last observed, he'd been tending the vegetable patch - and, coming without prior warning on Sohrab Quine, have some sort of fit. Feeling that that my place was beside her, I went, too.

The pause that followed our re-entrance was long and strained. Jez, the sidekick, had occupied one of the armchairs and apparently gone to sleep. Quine and the blonde, who had taken up a position on the sofa, were...I won't say 'canoodling', but the next best thing to it. And Clara, on the other armchair, her hands round her knees and her face a ghastly white, looked like she was modelling for a canvas called *'The Dying Teenager'.*

"So, Mr Quine, you're a lecturer at Nork, I believe?" said Mum, sounding flustered and rather too breezy.

Quine looked up and ran a chunky hand through his hair.

"Uh-huh, I do some lecturing there. But not for much longer, I hope."

I noticed Clara tense up.

"No?" said Mum.

"No way. I mean, do you know what it's like, being a big fish in a small pond?" asked Quine.

"It's wet? Crowded? Uncomfortable?" I suggested. Once more he ignored me. He'd meant the remark rhetorically, I suppose.

"I'm planning a move, maybe to Goldsmith's or The Slade; maybe to the States. Y'know, somewhere with more *profile*," he said, tossing his chunky hair and showing us his own chunky profile - of which you would have thought that he had more than enough already. "The thing is, once this Ronnie Bastard project is under way, the Art World will be my oyster," he added.

And no doubt he was right, for as far as the Media were concerned, this new chalk figure would give them just the sort of *succès de scandale* which they looked to Art for. Quine would be a nine day's wonder, at least, and nine days would be enough for him to make whatever career moves he wished to make. This was the conclusion I was coming to, when the door was pushed open and, as Fate would have it, in came Dad.

He must have known who Quine was by instinct. At any rate, he froze, stared at Quine, then at Jez, then back at Quine, then at Fliss, then at Clara. I saw her begin to mouth the words, "This is Sohrab", but Dad got in first.

"I have a feeling you must be Sohrab Quine," he said. He was trying to sound firm and straight-to-the-point, I could tell, but at the same time you couldn't help noticing that his voice was a touch quavery.

"And you must be Clara's Dad. Hi, Clara's Dad," drawled Quine.

"Clara has told us all about your latest project."

"Yeah?" returned Quine, with what I think was meant to be a look of modesty. At any rate, he raised a single chunky eyebrow and bent a few chunky forehead lines above it, as though preparing to say: "Well, y'know, 'genius' is an over-used word..."

"So, tell me - this figure you intend to carve...how do you plan to *characterize* him?"

Quine frowned. "I don't quite get you..."

"I mean, how do you intend to make him recognizable as, what's he called? Ronnie Bastard? - when, so far as I know, there's no Ronnie Bastard iconography?"

"'No Ronnie Bastard iconography...'" Quine repeated, chuckling. "I like it. No, well, maybe there isn't - but Ronnie's got his own logo, y'know. You haven't seen it? Well, he's playing a sawn-off synth-guitar in front of this wheel of lights. It's something like that old Shiva picture

75

Clara told me about. In fact, now I come to think of it, I guess it was that similarity that made me think of doing Ronnie in the first place. And that's how we're going to do him: playing his guitar with the wheel behind him." Quine acted out the latter image by fingering an imaginary instrument. "Hey, and did I tell you, Clara? Ronnie got my e-mail about it and he's really pleased. He's drying out after touring Japan and can't come out to the site, but he's invited me to come out and see him. 'Anytime,' he said, 'Anytime,' - so Fliss 'n me are going over tomorrow."

"How nice for you," said Dad. "He lives near here, then?"

"Yeah, quite near, quite near. He's got a big place out by Farnham."

"Really? Then for a nihilist he must live in some style."

"Yeah...yeah, I guess so," said Quine with another frown. He seemed to be cottoning on at last to the fact that Dad's mood was not altogether cordial.

"But I still don't quite understand why you have chosen to, as you put it, 'do Ronnie Bastard'?" Dad went on. "I can see that the likeness of his logo to the image of Shiva might have made you think of him, but what exactly made you feel that what England needs is a gigantic image of this... this *pop star* cut into the Downs?"

"Because he's a symbol for my generation, man. He's an icon of the tribe. And also because I'm being offered lots of bucks to put him on your local hill. Those Millennium Commissioners, *man*..." added Quine, smiling in a very post-modern, multi-choice way. That's to say, he could

76

have meant: "Those Commissioners - what a great bunch of guys," or "Those Commissioners - am I crazy or are they?" or anything in between. The choice was up to you and you could take your pick.

Dad began to pace up and down. Jez had begun to snore. Mum, meanwhile, was handing round the tea.

"But what about the figure of Shiva? How *can* you just destroy it?"

Quine sat up and leant forward. "You mean, the figure of Shiva which *you* say is there? Well, nobody else does, man."

"As a matter of fact, I do. I saw it with my own eyes," I put in.

Quine ignored me again. "And even if it is there, what's the big deal? You can't go on living in the past. Everyone knows that."

I could see Dad making one last effort to keep himself under control, but the words came tumbling out of his mouth as he half-shouted: "And are you seriously trying to tell me that this...this *pop logo* is on a par with the symbol of…of the *Lord of the Dance*?"

"I'm not trying to tell you anything, man," said Quine magnanimously. "I'm an artist. I create images, and whether you like them or not is up to you. That's your privilege. As for comparing Ronnie to Shiva, well, I guess it's just a case of *autres temps, autres whatevers*. People who've been to Ronnie's gigs kind of think that he's a Lord of the Dance too, know what I mean? Anyway, thanks for the tea, man. C'mon Fliss, Jez." He stood up and kicked Jez awake, then added: "You coming, Clara? We could use you to show us the way."

Clara didn't reply, but she slipped out of the room in the others' wake looking more uncomfortable than I had ever seen her look before. A few moments later we heard the sound of the convertible starting up, and saw through the sitting room window the car heading off down the drive with Clara in the back of it, lost to us.

The Junipers

It had been a confrontation about which Dad must have
dreamed since he'd first heard of Quine's new project the day
before. Somehow, though, I doubted whether it had gone
off quite as he'd imagined it. A mixture of diffidence and
stifled anger, the need to play the host, and embarrassment
in front of his children had cramped his style - though
what had really undone him, I guess, had been Quine's hip
indifference. "Hell," Quine had seemed to be saying, "You,
with your hide-bound, old-fashioned ideas, don't want *me*
to create a work of art, while I'm perfectly prepared to let
you think whatever thoughts you like. You're judging me,
man, while I'm not judging you at all."

Anyway, Dad shuffled out of the room looking more like
a ghost of Dad than Dad in person. I thought: "Well, it's up
to me. I'd better go to *The Junipers* now and see what's what.
The least I can do is try."

So, telling Mum I was going out for a cycle ride, I followed
Quine's car down our short, dishevelled gravel drive and
out on to the lane. I then cut across the well-worn path
through the bracken - passing as I did so a middle-aged
blind man with his dog, both regular features of the area
- and came out on the other lane, the one that ran up to
Woodcote Hill. At first you passed a few houses, then you
came out on heath land and birch woods. Finally, you came
to two more houses, large ones, set back among the trees.

The one on the left was called *Woodcote Lodge* and belonged to some people with whom we had a slight acquaintance: I'd been at school with their son. The one on the right at the end of the lane was *The Junipers*.

The first thing I saw was that someone was in residence. The gates were open, likewise the front and rear doors of a car in the drive and the front, double-doors of the house itself. Concluding that there couldn't be any savage guard dogs about if the gates were open, I rode inside and left my bike against the garage door. As to what I was going to say, though - I was still waiting for inspiration. Perhaps the best thing would be to pretend to be an emissary of Dad's in quest of the Bastable, and to rely on the occupier's not knowing about the intrigue which surrounded it.

As it turned out, no subterfuge was necessary. Or not at first, at least. As I came up to the house, a stone-built Victorian pile with touches of the Romanesque, an overweight, sandy-haired, balding man came out with what, from its shape, I took to be a large mirror wrapped in a blanket.

"Ah, is it Rich?" he exclaimed, peering short-sightedly in my direction. I hadn't a clue what he meant, but his manner was amiable enough.

"Or is it, ah, Dickon? Yes, it must be Dickon. I know your father said you might cycle over - "

"My name's Dan."

The man frowned. "I don't remember a Dan. A Rich and a Dickon, now - I remember those, but I don't recollect a Dan." He put the mirror on the back seat of the car, then put on a pair of glasses and looked at me closely.

"No..." He stepped to one side and briefly scrutinized my profile. "No...I've never seen you before in my life," he pronounced in a satisfied tone.

"Nor I you, sir," I replied. "And so far, so good," I thought, for he still sounded affable. But what was I to say next? I began a little tentatively: "It's just that I live down the road, and..."

"My dear fellow! No need to explain. It's simply that I mistook you for a son of the man who's bought this place."

"*Bought* it? You mean, it's been sold?" I exclaimed, for it hadn't occurred to me that the house would have changed hands already, with Aitken-Sneath not yet cold in the grave. I'd vaguely imagined that sorting out the probate and putting houses on the market and finding a buyer and closing the deal took simply ages.

But no, it had been sold, and the uppermost thought in my mind was that this could make things much trickier. In any event, I was now faced with an unknown quantity.

"That's right. Quick, wasn't it?" The man felt in his pockets, found a packet of cheroots, took one out, and lit it. After a couple of puffs, he suddenly stretched out a hand. "The name's Nigel Aitken, by the way. I'm old James's nephew; I dropped the 'Sneath'."

"Dan Waterman," I said, shaking his hand.

"Yes, an extraordinary thing, quite extraordinary. He didn't even have a survey done. Didn't need to, since he was paying cash. But don't think I'm complaining," Mr Aitken went on. "I suppose that houses like this are much sought after...its location close to London, its view...but I can't really say it would be my cup of tea. Still, this Mandeville fellow - "

"Mandeville!" I exclaimed. "Did you say 'Mandeville'?"

"Yes. A Bryan Mandeville. He's bought the place - and most of the furniture, too. It hadn't been put on the market and, to tell you the truth, I hadn't made up my mind what to do with it - then along came this Mandeville chap and offered me a price which, frankly," he paused and looked from side to side, as though for fear of being overheard, "was over the odds. *Well* over the odds. So, what could I say, but yes, all right, if you want it, it's yours."

"And you thought I was one of his sons?"

"That's right, that's right. There are two, you know, and Mandeville said that one of them - though off-hand, I can't remember which - would cycle over here today. So, naturally, when I saw you with your bike, I assumed you were he. Until I put my glasses on, at least."

He began to turn back to the house and I began to fear that, thinking I was merely some curious local on no particular mission, he was about to bid me good-day. Somehow I had to keep the conversation going...

"So, Mr Mandeville's bought this house," I said, with the stress on 'Mandeville'.

"Yes. Why, do you know him?"

"I've met him once or twice. He was a colleague of my father's."

"Oh yes? He's some sort of historian, I believe. A historian and a bibliophile."

"A bibliophile? How do you mean?"

The man looked at his watch and began to walk towards the front door. "You will excuse me, I'm sure, but I've just got one or two things to clear out before this Mr Mandeville moves in. He's due tomorrow afternoon. Now, what were you saying? A bibliophile? Yes...he insisted on buying all the books in the house - of which there are a lot, I can tell you. My uncle - but that's another story. Yes, he's bought them all."

"That's funny," I said quickly, "Because I picked one up in the Oxfam Shop yesterday."

"Ah well, there were half a dozen books lying round - not in the shelves - and this Mandeville chappy said he didn't need those particular ones, so I let Mrs Petrie take them. She was the housekeeper here, you know. I suppose she must have thought the best thing to do was to give them to charity."

He was on the doorstep now, but there was still one other question that I wanted to ask.

"Tell me, sir, is there a priest's hole in this house. I once heard a story..." I said mendaciously.

"A priest's hole?"

"Yes, or a secret hiding place of some sort."

"Oh, good heavens, no. The house is much too late for priest's holes, you know. It's Victorian," he said, slapping the brick pillar beside the door, "and it would have to be centuries older if you wanted to find a priest's hole here. As for secret hiding places - it's a romantic notion, but all I can say is that *I* haven't found any."

I thanked the man and returned to my bike, while summarizing what I'd learned. The main thing was that, so far as I could tell, the Bastable manuscript had not yet been found. Aitken didn't appear to be aware of it, nor did he know of any secret hiding place. Mandeville, meanwhile, hadn't yet had the chance to search the house thoroughly. That at least was my assumption, and it seemed a safe one - but from tomorrow, when he moved in, it would be safe no longer. And the fact that he'd bought the house so swiftly - with his recent inheritance, no doubt - *and* had insisted on buying the books as well, showed just how much the proof of the Chalk Giant's existence meant to him.

I got on my bike and rode out through the gates. As I did so, another cyclist came in through them. He was kitted out with black lycra cycle pants, striped lycra top, shades, and futuristic, streamlined helmet - all the works, in fact - and, if it wasn't my imagination, he gave me a hard look as he passed.

Clara's Reappraisal

When I got back, the first person I saw was Clara. She was standing at the foot of the staircase, still looking sheepish, though no longer angry.

"You're home early," I said. I had assumed that she would still be out with her pals.

"Yes. I just showed them how to get to the hill, then came back."

As this was more or less the longest sentence she had spoken to me of her own free will for several weeks - or the longest uncritical sentence, at least - I felt emboldened to go on.

"Surely Quine must have been there before?"

"Yes, but not from this direction."

There was a pause. Clara continued to hover, one hand on the newel post.

"So, that was the great Sohrab Quine," I said. It was a little contentious, I know, but I felt that she wanted to talk.

In reply, however, she merely gave a sort of grunt. Not an impatient grunt or an aggressive grunt, but quite a ladylike one, and with a sigh at the end. I took this obscure response to mean: "Yes, that was indeed Sohrab Quine. But it's possible, just possible, that I'm having to reappraise the 'great'. Still, I don't know quite what I feel, yet."

I replied with a sympathetic "Yeah, well..."

There was another pause and then, much to my surprise, she said:

"Did you...did you do anything about that letter?"

"Yes, as a matter of fact I did." And what an opportunity to tell her about my detective work, I thought - then I reconsidered. I didn't want to risk losing her attention, and besides, the facts spoke for themselves. "I found out who wrote it," I said.

"Oh, yes?"

"It was the guy who lived at *The Junipers*."

"*The Junipers*? Oh, you mean the guard dog man."

"That's the one. He wrote it. Only then he went and died."

"He died? Oh...well, I guess that rather spoils it, then."

"It does and it doesn't," I said. "I don't think the guard dog man would have played ball, somehow, so maybe it's just as well that he's out of the picture. But get this: he died about three weeks ago, yet before the new owner had even decided whether to put *The Junipers* on the market or not, along came a Mr X and offered to buy the place for far more than it's worth - *the books included*."

"That's strange..."

"You're telling me. And guess who Mr X is?"

"I don't know. How should I know? Unless...unless it's Mandeville."

"You've got it in one. It's Mandeville. Which shows just how keen he is to get his grubby hands on the Bastable manuscript."

"Yes, I suppose it does..."

"But he hasn't got it yet."

"Oh? What makes you think that?"

"Because he hasn't moved into the house yet."

"Well, yes, I guess that makes sense." Clara made a half-interested *moue*. Then she frowned. "But isn't there someone there at present? I mean, mightn't the guard dog man's executors have found the book?"

"Aitken-Sneath - that's the guard dog man - left *The Junipers* to his nephew, and I've just come from talking to him. He knows nothing of any hiding place and seemed completely unsuspicious as to Mandeville's motives. So, no, I don't think he can have heard of the Bastable book. In fact, it wouldn't surprise me if there are only three living people who have. Mandeville, myself, and..."

I let my words tail off deliberately. Clara looked about three-quarters interested by now, and if possible I wanted her to fill in the dots herself. She didn't, but at least she added a few more of her own.

"And...?" she said in a puzzled voice.

"And *you*, Clara. And *you*."

"Well, yes, I guess that could be so. So what are you going to do now?"

I paused for a moment. The back door was open and I could just catch the sound of our parents' voices. They were too far off to hear what we were saying, but to be on the safe side I went over and shut the kitchen door. Then I gritted my teeth and said in my best tough guy voice:

"There's only one thing I can do. I have to break into *The Junipers* and look for the Bastable's hiding place."

87

Clara gave me an appraising look and a short, whistled "Phew!"

"What's more, I've got to do it tonight."

"You can't. The Smith-Enderbys are coming."

I started to protest, but of course she was right. They *were* coming, and I would have to be present. I cursed, yet inside myself I felt relieved. Somehow, I didn't fancy the idea of snooping round *The Junipers* after dark, even assuming I could get in and didn't set off any alarms. With the spiky ironwork on its roof, its dark, fake-Romanesque windows, its neglected, brooding air (for Aitken-Sneath could hardly have kept more than three or four rooms in daily use, and it was a sizeable, seven or eight-bedroomed house, at least) and its surrounding ring of conifers, the place was enough to give anyone the creeps in the day-time, let alone at night.

My plan had been to go towards dusk, or in other words, after supper - yet not so late that it would arouse Mum's and Dad's suspicions. By that time, I'd reasoned, Dickon (or Rich) should have gone, for the boy on the bike hadn't had any luggage with him and it seemed unlikely that he'd be staying the night. Of course, I could now put this plan into operation later. I could simply wait until after our guests had gone - and after I was supposed to be asleep - but the thought of a nocturnal raid on that shadowy house was altogether too much for me. Besides, if my absence from home were to be discovered, the questions asked afterwards would just be too awkward.

And if that sounded feeble, well - hell, I was a poet, not a housebreaker!

"Okay then, I'll go tomorrow. Tomorrow, early. The man I talked to, Aitken-Sneath's nephew, said that Mandeville moves in tomorrow afternoon. One of his sons is there just now, but he should be gone by this evening, and I'll have the place all to myself."

I laid a lot of stress on 'myself' in the hope that even at this late stage my sister might say: "You can't do it by yourself! I'm afraid that's quite impossible! You're my little brother and I feel responsible for you! *I'll* come, too." What she said instead was:

"Look, do you have a moment?"

"Sure, I think I can manage that."

"Well, the thing is...the thing is - let's go up to my room," she said, suddenly tiring of the cramped space at the foot of the stairs, as indeed I was myself. We went up to her room and she threw open a window, thus reducing the girlish fug of *Body Shop* perfume and takeaway pizza by a degree or two. She then stared out towards the fruit trees by the drive. There was an apple tree on one side, a pear tree on the other.

"I guess it was seeing them here - you know, where I've grown up - that's made me think that, well, maybe Sohrab's project isn't such a good idea," she said at last.

"'Such a good idea'? Who said it *was* such a good idea?"

"Well, I did for one. But I guess I never really thought it, you know, in *detail*. It was just that...you know, Dad's thing seemed so *hopeless* - "

"And this was your revenge on Fate?"

She thought about that for a moment. "Well, partly. But Sohrab's very convincing. He's *very* convincing. He's got this sort of *aura* about him and if you don't agree with him - I mean, maybe not on some specific point, but with his general attitude - you find yourself feeling you must be really out of touch. You feel like your eyes just haven't been opened and you want him to open them, just like he says he can. The course he teaches is called *'Opening Our Eyes'*, you know. Yet the funny thing is that, when he does open them, it's sort of like everything you used to see as interesting and beautiful seems just *uncool* - you know what I mean? It's very confusing."

"And you're confused?"

She nodded, though with some difficulty. Her head seemed to loop round in a circle while she frowned, then at last it went up and down.

I didn't know what to say. On the one hand, there seemed so much that I could have said. For example, I could have offered her a critique of Quine that was a lot more searching than her own, presenting him as the bumptious opportunist that, for my money, he was. But at this early juncture such remarks would have been a bit ambitious. Or I could have said, looking round her room, "These Ronnie Bastard C.D.s - this black bomber jacket - these rusty metal constructions, made out of nails and lager cans, which you created, if 'created' is the word, when you gave up your carving of Shiva - that Brit Art poster on the wall - etc., etc. - why not light a bonfire in the garden and chuck them on it?" But that also might have been too much, as yet.

At any rate, I was mulling over these points when she turned to me and said:

"About tomorrow. I'll come with you, if you like."

The Smith-Enderbys

I suppose that every family has their Smith-Enderbys. Zena, the female of the duo, was a cousin of Mum's with a compulsive need to keep in touch. This took the form not simply of the annual Christmas card but also of the half-yearly typed report on the progress, deeds and achievements of her wonder-family, together with a tendency to drop in out of the blue, or almost out of the blue, at awkward moments.

Apparently, she had once been sane enough, but years of being married to Mark Smith-Enderby, a small businessman, had completely turned her mind. Of course, that was my view of the matter - and a view, I was increasingly coming to realise, shared by Mum and Dad - but in their own opinion I'm sure they both thought themselves absolutely normal. Indeed, Clara's pet name for them was 'The Normals'.

Also, when I say that Mr Smith-Enderby was a 'small businessman', I doubt whether this is a description he would have chosen himself. For one thing he wasn't small, but of more or less medium height, and, for another, he ran a chain of jeweller's shops in the Croydon area. In addition to that, he had his fingers - as he never tired of telling us - in a number of pies. He meant, of course, in other businesses, but his use of those words always made me look at his fingers themselves, which were freckled and stubby, and think of those pies, whose golden, glazed pastry he was so happily making a mess of, and the image wasn't a pleasant one. His conversation consisted largely of financial tips and advice on pension schemes, etc., usually prefaced by the phrases, "If I were you, Ned," or "Here's a good thing, Ned," and peppered with racy anecdotes from the world of Buildings and House Contents Insurance. Zena's conversation, on the other hand, revolved around her children - and here it always seemed to me unfortunate that she should have had two, one a girl of about Clara's age, and one a boy more or less of mine. Alana's and Bradley's exploits, contrasted with our own, were so exciting, their prospects so extraordinary, their achievements already so striking, that - had you taken all that Mrs Smith-Enderby said at face value - you could have come away from an audience with her feeling small to the point of insignificance. You might even have felt, "Why bother?"

I'd have to be Jane Austen, I suppose, to do full justice to the chit-chat at dinner that evening - but I'm not, and at the same time I can't help feeling that their visit was like a boring chapter in a good book. It interrupted the story. Still, as we ate our way through the dessert course there was an exchange which is relevant to my tale. It went something like this, with Mrs Smith-Enderby speaking:

"What did you say this was called, Laura?"

"Pouding Alsacien," said Mum.

"Mmm," responded the other, visibly chewing. "It's most interesting. Of course, Alana's well into her Cordon Bleu course at Prue Leith's. The things that girl can do with a lemon, an egg and a pint of sour cream - you'd be amazed!"

Mum could only manage an "Oh, ah, really?" in reply, but it didn't matter, because at this point Mark Smith-Enderby took over.

"Tell me, Ned, what are you doing with yourself these days?" he inquired.

I felt my father tense up, and understandably so. It was the sort of question which a man of his nature dislikes at the best of times, and this was far from being the best of times. Probably he would have liked to say, "Well, this morning I felt real delight, if only for a moment, in looking at a dwarf lily which I planted last year and which has just come into flower, and generally speaking I try to hold the family together..." or words to that effect; but these unofficial, unquantifiable, untaxable things were hardly what Mr Smith-Enderby had in mind. I knew that and Dad knew that.

"Oh...a little writing, a little campaigning," said Dad finally.

"Campaigning?" queried Zena.

"Yes. I must have mentioned our discovery, I'm sure."

"Your discovery?" asked Mark, through a mouthful of *pouding*.

"The Chalk Giant on our doorstep. I'm sure I've mentioned it before."

Mark Smith-Enderby looked over his shoulder towards the back door, as though hoping - or fearing - to see a Chalk Giant there. Then he must have remembered something, for the blank, worried look disappeared from his face as he said:

"Oh, yes I do remember something about it, though the details escape me. You thought you'd discovered some... half a mo., don't tell me...some *prehistoric* thingummy, wasn't it?"

Mum answered, explaining patiently, if a little nervously, all about the sighting of the chalk figure, how Dad believed it to be of Shiva and that it must have been carved on Woodcote Hill some umpteen centuries back, perhaps by Phoenicians or perhaps by Celts, and how this lost image, this great and beautiful lost image, was being threatened by a destruction more absolute than that of time and weather.

Mum had often played the devil's advocate to Dad, but now that she was conveying his ideas on his behalf, we saw what she really felt, and gradually her careworn face became transfigured, her words touched with inspiration.

About mid-way through her explanation, however, Mark Smith-Enderby began to look bemused. Judging by her expression, his wife's bemusement took longer to develop, but once it did so, it quickly became complete. There was a long silence, then Mark said at last:

"Ah well, it all sounds rather a lost cause."

"Yes, I suppose it does," said Dad.

"And there can't have been any money in it, anyway. I mean, if you *owned* the hill, now, it might have paid you to get a grant to restore this, ah, image, and then charge the Great British Public to watch the restoration at close quarters... Yes, that *might* have been possible...though if the image is as big as you say it is, I suppose it'd be visible from a goodish distance - and that would make the remunerative side of it rather tricky... No, it's a difficult one, a difficult one, whichever way you look at it."

"I never planned to make money out of it," said Dad.

"No? Really? Well, I dare say you wanted to make some sort of splash in the academic world, and that could have translated into more of the folding stuff. I mean, don't tell me that that never crossed your mind?"

Dad looked as though he was about to deny this, then changed his mind.

"Well, perhaps you're right," he said.

The funny thing was that his guest, while overlooking - or indeed, *by* overlooking - the complexities and subtleties of the case, had put his stubby, freckled finger right on something which Dad seemed not to have thought of before.

"Yes, perhaps you're right," he repeated. "I suppose... I suppose I *did* rather hope to make my reputation out of that discovery, yes. Perhaps that was rather a selfish way of looking at it."

He was talking to his *pouding* as much as to the Smith-Enderbys, which was just as well, for I couldn't help seeing Mark look at Zena as though to say, "For goodness' sake, where's the off switch?"

Meanwhile, Dad went on musing aloud. "Yes...I suppose I was seeing it only partly in terms of it's...its deeper meaning, and partly in terms of what it could do for my career. And I'll tell you another thing. All the time I was writing *The Chalk Man*, I found myself really torn between wanting to be as dry and non-committal as possible in order to keep in with my colleagues, and wanting to say, 'Look, there's an extraordinary message here on this hill, left to us by people who knew something we've long forgotten. More than that, it's a *symbol* - it can have real power, if only we're receptive to it.' He spooned up a mouthful of *pouding* reflectively. 'And I suppose the thought of fame, even academic fame, was rather entrancing, too...'

"But after all, what's fame? It's just a puff of smoke, a phantasm," said Clara dismissively.

We were all somewhat surprised by this, I think, and Dad almost laughed.

"A 'phantasm'? Did you say 'a phantasm'?" he inquired.

Clara said that yes, she had, and what of it?

"Oh, nothing. It's just that, though I've seen it in books, it's the first time in my life I've heard the word used conversationally."

Mark Smith-Enderby was still looking for that off switch - in fact, he virtually had his hand on Dad's back now, feeling for the button - when his wife came to the rescue. She started to say in an overloud voice that, yes, she'd had to cope with the same sort of disappointment when Bradley, at his last School Sports Day, had come second in the 100 metres when all his friends and admirers, including - she had had it on good authority - the headmaster himself, had expected him to win it. But just as she was getting to the meat of the story, which had to do with the words of wisdom imparted to her by a counsellor friend of hers - my mother, who couldn't have been listening, cut in with:

"All the same, I don't think you should give up, Ned. When you and Dan saw that vision - if that's not too strong a word - it created an *event*. And, well, one feels that the ramifications of an event like that have to be gradually gone through, and that that takes time. Maybe the conclusion that it's best not to think of such things in terms of personal success and fame and so on, is just one of those ramifications. Another could be that you've now seen who your friends are - and who they aren't..."

She went on in this vein for some time, as though speaking from beyond herself - while the Smith-Enderby's search for the off switch became ever more frantic. Soon afterwards, the party broke up - our guests went off to their Spanish-style villa out Croydon way - and I began to feel that, with Mum's comforting words, Dad's long crisis had entered a different phase, and one that - who knows? - might yet end well.

The Break-in

But I didn't feel quite so confident the next day, as Clara and I strolled with an affected casualness past the gates of *The Junipers*.

We'd meant to leave home much earlier, but what with one thing and another it just hadn't happened. For one thing, being a Saturday, there'd been various household chores to do. For another, I think we'd both felt so conscious of the criminality that our expedition was going to involve, that In an instinctive kind of way we'd resorted to the guise of appearing relaxed, laid back and in no hurry to do anything. There was another factor to be taken into consideration, too. So rarely did we do things together these days that if we'd announced we were 'going for a walk', we'd only have drawn more attention to ourselves than we wanted.

So, Clara went off by herself and I, having told Mum and Dad that I was going to the Downs, followed after her some twenty minutes later. We met where the lane forked and continued up towards *The Junipers* together. Our plan was to check that the place looked deserted as we passed the entrance, and then to break through the wire fence where the guard dog signs were.

The house certainly looked unoccupied. The gates were shut, there were no cars present in the drive, and no signs of life behind the windows. But of course not all of the house was visible from the lane, and it might have been a different story could we have seen the back of the house or the offices at the side. Besides, even when Aitken-Sneath had been in residence, the place had hardly had a lively air. Still, we had to take our chances and we both felt that, for the moment, *The Junipers* was empty.

A certain excitement spurred us on as well. The prospect of lifting the Bastable manuscript from under Bryan Mandeville's nose had its entertaining side, fraught with danger though it was. It ranked as a *caper*, and a caper was always to be recommended.

Of course, had we gone into all the ins and outs of what we were about to do, we might have paused - for, looked at from a strictly ethical point of view, breaking into someone's house, poking round at will and robbing it of a precious commodity, just wasn't done: at least, not under normal circumstances. But these weren't normal circumstances, and in any case we weren't planning to pinch the Bastable, merely to borrow it. When we'd found the proof we needed, we would happily return it - either by the method we were about to put into practice now, or by leaving it in a brown paper wrapper inside the gates, or even by sending it through the post.

Now, the fact that we were intending to return it had made me acutely conscious of the need to beware of leaving fingerprints behind, and I'd insisted that we both wore gloves. Mine were some thin cotton workman's ones which I'd found in the garden shed; Clara's were of off-white lace and had been a gift from an aunt a year or two back. Since it was round about then that she'd started on her 'black period', this could well have been the first time she'd worn them.

I'd wanted her to wear a hairnet, too, on the grounds that a single bright red hair from her head, if left at *The Junipers*, might later lead the police to the thieves. Her reply, however, had been:

"Don't be ridiculous."

In saying this, there had been a certain grim derring-do about her manner that had been encouraging, if faintly worrying, and I hadn't tried to argue with her.

We passed the gates and continued on towards Woodcote Hill. After a few yards, the lane petered out into a bridle path. A few yards after that, another, narrower path branched off to the right. It ran between the grounds of *The Junipers* on the one side and a high bank crowned with evergreens on the other. On the former side, the broken-glass-topped wall continued for a short stretch, then gave way to the barbed wire fence beyond which was the dark wood of box trees by which Clara and I had often been intrigued.

We reached the barbed wire fence and stopped. The grounds of *The Junipers* were roughly square in shape, and of its four sides, one (where the gates were) was bordered by the high brick wall, another (on the opposite side to us) also marked the edge of the demesne next door, and a third looked out onto the open hill. The wall was too high to climb without a ladder: at least, by the likes of us; the route through someone else's grounds appeared too dangerous; and the lower side of the square, on the hilltop, was too exposed. Which all meant that the weakest point of *The Junipers'* defences was right here, where we stood.

Breathing fast, our ears attuned to the sounds about us, we looked at one another while I pulled the wire-cutters out of my pocket. The fence was about five feet high, and though it would have been possible - with sufficient care - to have climbed it, the quickest way to get from *A*, where we were, to *B*, where we wanted to be, would be by cutting the wire. Besides, I'd often read of Prisoners of War doing this and had always wanted to try it myself.

Of course, there was one big difference between ourselves and the men who'd been stuck in Colditz, etc. Apart from the fact that they had been in Nazi Germany, and we were in peacetime Surrey, I mean. And this was that, while they'd been trying to break *out*, we were trying to break *in*.

There was no-one coming, nor any sound of anyone coming. There were a number of paths leading out onto Woodcote Hill, and in any case, most people who came along the lane past *The Junipers* stayed on the bridle path. The narrowness and gloom of the footpath we had chosen and the threatening character of Aitken-Sneath's signs, not to mention the barbed wire, generally put them off.

I clipped a wire. I clipped another. Then I said:

"Do you think this is okay?"

"Oh, get on with it. If you want a moral philosopher, look in *Yellow Pages*," snapped Clara. It was a whispered snap, however.

"I suppose you're right," I murmured.

"Of course I'm right. And hurry up with it."

I hurried, but the trouble with using wire cutters was that it would make it rather obvious that someone had broken into *The Junipers'* grounds. Still, the odds on Sherlock Holmes or Miss Marple coming down the path within the next half-hour, observing the cut wire, deducing from the freshness of the wire at the breaks that it had just been done, and having the gumption or foolhardiness to follow us inside, were remote.

I clipped away at the strands of wire and pushed the loose pieces apart. Still, no-one came. All well and good, then...except that at this point I started feeling very doubtful about what lay ahead. How on earth were we to find the secret hiding place - assuming there really was one - and the Bastable within it, assuming it was there - in half an hour, or an hour, or a week? The house was huge, we'd never been in it, we wouldn't know where to start. However, the thought of Mandeville's underhand behaviour made me feel more resolute. The least we could do was try.

I cut one more strand, then Clara climbed through. I followed her and tried to push the wire back into place so that the gap wouldn't be too obvious. Then I heard a noise.

The noise of someone approaching.

He or she was coming up the path - that is, from the hill side - and it sounded as though they had a dog with them. They weren't in sight yet - but then, nor was I out of sight. The trouble was that the box grove where I now was afforded little shelter. The trees grew fairly close together, but their trunks were thin and there wasn't any undergrowth. You had to go some distance back up the slope before you reached the safety of a clump of rhododendrons. It was to them that Clara had hurried, and I could just see her bright red head disappearing among the dark green, shiny leaves. But whoever was coming was getting closer now and I had no time in which to follow her. I didn't know what to do: I could hear the dog sniffing its way up the muddy path. If I dropped to the ground, I was bound to be seen. If I scurried behind the nearest tree, my legs would show up. If I stood stock-still, I couldn't be missed - but at least I wouldn't look as though I were trying to hide.

I stood stock-still. The dog appeared and started scuffling around by the spot where we'd stood while I'd clipped the wire. It was a Labrador. Then the dog's owner appeared.

It was the blind man.

I almost laughed aloud with relief. But I didn't - and I didn't move, either, since I'd read that blind people's hearing was particularly acute. The dog saw me and looked at me curiously, but didn't do anything. The man said, "Come on, Rover" and continued up the path. The dog followed.

I waited for a moment, then hurried on through the rank-smelling box grove and joined my sister.

"What happened?"

"It's okay. It was the blind man."

"That was a stroke of luck."

"Not luck. Fate." I felt suddenly optimistic. Things were going to go well and I let Clara's snort of scepticism pass unchallenged.

We struggled through the rhododendrons and came out by a stagnant, rectangular lily pond, covered with green slime. Beyond this was a fair-sized lawn. In Aitken-Sneath's time the grounds must have been well looked after, but in the three weeks since he had died the grass could not have been cut nor the herbaceous borders weeded nor the roses on the terrace dead-headed. It had been rainy, too, and the grass had grown fast, half-covering the croquet hoops that were planted in it. Beyond the lawn, the terrace had a neglected air. Beyond the terrace, the house lowered.

I've described it already as a stone-built Victorian house with Romanesque touches, but that's not to tell the half of it. For 'Victorian' read 'High Victorian', for 'Romanesque' read 'round-headed windows with gargoyles on the mullions', and don't forget to throw in a curving French roof topped with lots of spiky bits of ironwork and pierced with what looked like portholes, several tall chimneys and the odd Corinthian capital. In other words, it was one big stylistic hotchpotch with 'nouveau riche' as good as written all over it. Also, to the side of the terrace, there was an enormous conservatory.

Everything was quiet. We hovered at the edge of the rhododendrons for a long while, watching the house and waiting, I suppose, for each other to make the first move. Then, without a word being said, we circumnavigated the lily pond, crossed the ragged lawn together and reached the terrace. This was a few feet higher than the lawn and we crouched down below the stone balustrade which ran along its edge.

Peering over, we looked towards the tall windows nearest us. There was still no sign of movement within the house, but I felt that, before we moved any closer, a little experiment might be a good idea. Picking a stone out of the rose bed beyond the balustrade, I threw it at one of the windows. I had meant to make a noise which, if there *was* anyone in the house, would attract their attention and warn us of their presence. But in my nervousness I must have flung it too hard, for with what seemed an ear-splitting *crash!* it smashed its way straight through one of the panes.

"I thought we'd come here to rob the place, not to smash it up," said Clara dryly.

I explained what I'd meant to do. "If there's anyone around, they're bound to come and investigate."

But no-one did investigate, and after a further couple of minutes we crossed the terrace and went up to the window through which I'd thrown the stone. To compound the house's stylistic jumble, the room inside had a painted ceiling in a kind of neo-classical vein. A large sideboard stood against one wall; a suite of chairs and a sofa occupied the centre of the room.

"Mandeville must have bought the furniture in case the manuscript is hidden in it. It could be in that sideboard, for instance," I murmured.

Clara nodded, adding that we hadn't got all day in which to stand here talking.

"Look - it's half past eleven already."

"Oh well, we should have until two o'clock at least," I said. "Anyway, these windows look pretty secure. Let's try the conservatory."

The latter turned out to be in need of some repair. A number of the roof panes had fallen in and one of the glass wall panels was cracked right across. Weeds had grown up in the miniature, half empty pool within, while rain had collected on an object of quite surpassing ugliness - a grotto of a lumpy, pitted, grey stone which looked to be artificial but which, I found out later, was actually aerated, volcanic rock. Several fragments of broken glass were scattered on the Minton tile floor.

To these fragments Clara added some more by pushing at the cracked pane with her foot. Both halves fell in and shattered into further pieces. The space now cleared was large enough for us to climb through - just.

Once inside, we went over to the door which led into the house. It proved to be locked. The upper part was panelled with glass, however, and I was just about to adopt my sister's method and smash it - in order, if possible, to then reach inside and turn the lock - when Clara said:

"Wait. Sometimes people leave a key around...you know, in case they get locked out."

The obvious place to look was under a medium-sized flowerpot beside the door. I lifted it, and - amazingly - there was a key underneath.

We tried it and it worked; the door opened and, presto! we were inside the house.

The Search

"Right, I vote we look in the library first," I said. "It's possible that Aitken-Sneath simply left the Bastable among his other books, and we mustn't overlook the obvious."

"Okay. If there is a library."

There was. It was on the ground floor at the side of the house, through the large sitting room - the one with the sideboard - and we were lucky enough to find it straightway.

The trees grew close to the house here, and the panelled room's share of sunlight was meagre. Bookshelves occupied the best part of three of the walls. I took one wall, Clara another.

"What are we looking for, exactly?" she asked.

"I'm not sure," I said, running a finger along the spines of the books on the top shelf. "Something that's pretty ancient-looking, I guess. I mean, if it's a Seventeenth Century manuscript, that makes it between three and four hundred years old. But whether it's bound or not, and, if it is, whether the binding's original or a recent replacement, we simply don't know."

"Well, there's nothing over here," said Clara.

I was more painstaking, but perhaps that was just because the books in front of me were older. There was a set of Gibbon, a set of Macaulay...a number of early travel books...a first edition of Doughty's *Arabia Deserta*...but nothing by anyone called Bastable.

The bookshelves on the third wall proved a blank, too. Of course, it was possible that Aitken-Sneath had disguised the Bastable as another book altogether, but this struck me as unlikely. In his letter, he'd spoken of a hiding place, and the suggestion was that it would be large enough to hold other valuables beside the manuscript. My guess, therefore, was that either Aitken-Sneath had had the hiding place made and had put the manuscript there - or he hadn't, in which case it was somewhere accessible, if not exactly to hand.

"Let's find his study. It could be there," said Clara.

Glad that she was beginning to take the initiative, I agreed. And we were lucky again, for the study proved to be connected to the library, through a door at right-angles to the one by which we had entered.

It, too, was a gloomy room. The shutters were pulled to, and the air smelt of furniture polish and dust, with maybe a trace of cologne.

Clara switched the light on. It was a small room containing a desk, another bookshelf, a leather-upholstered chaise longue, and a filing cabinet. There were no knick-knacks or paintings, rugs or objets d'art, for - as in the sitting room and library - all the smaller furnishings appeared to have been removed by Aitken junior. Presumably Mandeville had discounted them as possible containers for the manuscript, and had therefore not wanted to buy them.

I took the filing cabinet, Clara the desk. Both were not only unlocked but had the keys *in situ*, which surprised me. Maybe the reason was that, having searched through them, Aitken had believed their contents to be unimportant and had therefore left them unlocked for Mandeville's convenience. They were full of Aitken-Sneath's papers, though - which suggested that these, as well as the books, had been included in Mandeville's purchase.

Clara tipped a drawerful of such papers on the desk and started rifling through them.

"Don't make too much mess. We don't want Mandeville to know we've been here," I said.

"Okay, okay. Anyway, there's nothing really old here, and if there's a clue among this lot as to where he hid the book - well, we just haven't got time to read through it all."

She was right, and precisely the same was true of the material in the filing cabinet - though as far as I could tell it consisted entirely of dull but innocuous articles on local history, and correspondence about the same. I shut the cabinet up and went over to the bookshelf. Once again, the books all appeared to be what they said they were: volumes on the North Downs and Surrey, bound copies of the Parish News, and reference books.

I looked at Clara unhappily. She was putting the last of the papers back in the drawers.

"Any luck?"

"No, none at all."

"Well...there's his bedroom, I guess. We ought to look there."

She nodded, but I saw her looking at her watch, and doubtless the thought that was beginning to pump away like a Ronnie Bastard song in my head was pumping away in hers, too. It was that when I'd casually remarked that we had until two o'clock at least, I'd been wildly over-optimistic. True, Aitken had told me that Mandeville was moving in during the afternoon, but that may just have been a rough estimate. And if Mandeville should turn up now - or, worse, when we were upstairs, our line of retreat cut off - it would be about as awkward as you could get.

We stepped through a door in the corner of the study and found ourselves in a strange, top lit stairwell. Seven doors, each with ornate brass fingerplates and handles, opened onto this stairwell at equidistant intervals, and the red-carpeted stairs led up beneath a plaster relief of a cherub, then divided into two and ascended to a gallery. All around this gallery were further doors - one of which had to be the master bedroom.

The intense, unwelcoming silence - the openness of this well, which made us feel unpleasantly exposed - the watching eyes implied by all the keyholes and doors left ajar - the sense of being trapped in the heart of the house, yet unable to see outside, for apart from the skylight, there were no windows here...all this made me nervous, and if I wasn't mistaken, it made Clara nervous, too. We hesitated and for my part I felt tempted to run.

But the silence remained unbroken, and Clara started walking up the stairs. I followed, a few paces behind. She went left where the stairs forked, and I went right. We looked in the rooms as we came to them, and the second one that Clara tried was the one we wanted. It was situated above the sitting room and looked out beyond the rhododendrons and the box trees and the Weald to the South Downs - though these were scarcely visible now, for it had begun to rain.

The room was large, the bed a four poster. On top of the cabinet beside the bed were several numbers of *Country Life* and a copy of *Barchester Towers*. Clara went over to the built-in wardrobes; I looked inside the cabinet - which contained a water jug and glass - and then under the bed.

And then we heard a car.

One of the advantages of the house's isolated position, as far as I was concerned, was that there was no noise of traffic. Thus, when a car did roll up, you heard it - even when you were on the wrong side of the house and the windows were shut and, outside, the rain was pouring down.

Clara looked at her watch while my heart began to jump about like a one-legged clubber.

"It's half past twelve. If that's Mandeville, he's early."

It sounded cool enough, but no sooner had she said it than she slammed the wardrobe door and hared across the room and out through door and round to the far side of the gallery. I had the same idea: we would look out of one of the front bedroom windows and see whose car it was. And if it turned out to be the postman, say, we could rest easy and continue our search.

But it wasn't the postman. It was Mandeville.

We peered out from behind the net curtains and watched as a Range Rover with Mandeville at the wheel pulled up beneath us. He had his sons beside him, and - as we observed when he opened the door - he had an I'm-here-and-I-mean-business expression on his ugly mug. Brusquely, he got out of the car and then stepped back a few paces in order to gaze up at the house.

I imagine that his aim was to give the place a proprietary glance, as though he were posing for a Victorian painting. You know - *The First Day in the New Home* - that kind of thing. But as he looked up, so we ducked down, and therefore I did not actually see what he did.

The funny thing was that instead of getting the hell out of there, we both stayed by the window, waiting to see what happened next. I think we felt a horrid fascination which, together with an inertia induced by fear, seemed to render us unable to move. Bryan Mandeville did not strike me as the sort of man to give you a word of warning and a friendly pat on the head when he found you in his house. He would call in the cops for sure, and the ensuing embarrassment - let alone the unpleasantness - would be almost too much to bear. And yet there we were, waiting for the worst to happen.

However, the rattle of Mandeville's keys broke the spell, and in what seemed a single rapid movement we got up, ran out of the room, half-jumped down the stairs, and tore into the sitting room. At that point we heard the porch door slam and another door open - it must have been into the stairwell. We passed from the sitting room into the small anteroom into which we had first made our entrance, and thence through the back door into the conservatory. Clara slipped through where the broken pane had been and I slipped after her, catching my jumper on a piece of jagged glass as I did so. But at least we'd reached the terrace now…and now the lawn…and now the -

But at that point two boys come round the corner, saw us, and shouted in unison: "Hoy!"

The Confrontation

It was still raining, though not as much as it had been doing a moment ago, and not only did I feel awkward, I also felt distinctly wet.

"Who are you?" asked the first and slightly older-looking boy. He was about Clara's age, though in his height he took after his father and was a little shorter than me. He also took after his father in a certain bluntness of manner, for while "Who are you?" looks fairly harmless on the page and could be read as an amiable, puzzled inquiry, or even as an expression of wonder, when spoken on this occasion it was nothing short of a belligerent, stroppy demand.

It didn't get an answer, however, for it was instantly followed by a second question from the other boy. He was a year or so younger than me, and had gingery hair and a stocky frame. He was one of those people who hold their arms out from their sides, as though to say, "My biceps are so big, I couldn't get my arms to dangle down vertically even if I tried."

"Yeah, and what are you doing here?" he said in much the same tone of voice as that adopted by his brother.

Of course, these questions presented us with a ticklish problem. We didn't want to give our real names, in case the information should get back to Mandeville and he should put two and two together. We didn't want to give false names either, however - for being near neighbours, the truth about who we were would sooner or later be bound to come out. Nor, for obvious reasons, did we want to say, "Actually, we're burglars. We've been trying to half-inch the manuscript your old man thinks he's bought." To ignore the first question altogether seemed the best bet, therefore; but as for the second, "Just passing through" seemed a scarcely adequate reply - and to anyone who was at all acquainted with the grounds of *The Junipers* it was also an unconvincing one.

Anyway, I was standing there, getting wet and trying to think of a suitable story, when Clara said:

"We're looking for a tennis ball."

"A tennis ball?" repeated the second boy.

"Yes. We were on our way to play a game when my brother accidentally knocked a ball in here."

"What, tennis in the rain?" queried the first boy.

"It's just a shower, isn't it? It'll soon pass over."

"Anyway, you can't have been going to play on the hill - it slopes too much," said the first boy with a kind of sneer. He seemed to think he was some sort of police detective, like the ones you see on TV who are always giving people a hard time.

Mind you, he had a point. There weren't any tennis courts on Woodcote Hill, and I was just wondering how Clara was going to get out of that one when she said with a touch of hauteur:

"We're on our way to the Thompsons', as it happens. They live across the way, at *Woodcote Lodge*."

She was right, they did. They were the acquaintances I've mentioned before, the ones who owned the house across the lane from *The Junipers*, and although we'd never actually used their tennis court, I knew that they had one and that they'd told Mum and Dad we could use it if we wished. Clara's story seemed a good one, therefore, and I couldn't really see how these Mandeville brats could continue their interrogation without giving themselves a bad name in the neighbourhood. This didn't seem to have occurred to them, however, for the elder boy shared a disbelieving glance with the younger boy, then turned back to us and said:

"So where are your rackets, then?"

Clara sighed. It was almost a yawn. "We left them outside. You don't go clambering over people's fences with tennis rackets in your hand. It encumbers you," she replied.

"Does it?" said the second boy.

"Yes, it does."

"So, they're outside are they?" He walked over to the junipers which gave the house its name and that fringed the wall by the lawn. "I don't see them."

"That's hardly surprising," Clara replied coolly. "We hid them in the bushes in case nosey people should see them and pinch them." She emphasized the word 'nosey'. "And anyway, they're not there. They're further down. You can't get over the wall there."

The ginger-haired boy seemed to be about to say something in response to this, and I was beginning to

121

wonder if this inquiry into our non-existent game of tennis was going to go on indefinitely, when the older boy suddenly changed his tune.

"Hang on," he said, staring at me, "Haven't I seen you somewhere before?"

"I've really no idea," I said, but of course I had. He must have been the boy on the bike whom I'd passed after talking to Aitken. He'd been so disguised by his cycling gear, however, that I hadn't recognised him.

"Wait a minute...wait a minute. I saw you *here*, yesterday afternoon," he announced.

"Did you?"

"Yes..." He put his hands to his temples and looked down at the ground, as though to see into the past more clearly. "You weren't on foot, though. No...let me see...you were on a bike - that's right! You were on a bike...and you were *cycling away from this house.*" He took his hands from his head and looked at me with narrowed eyes.

"Your powers of memory are astonishing," I remarked.

"So - what were you doing here then? Not looking for another tennis ball, I suppose?"

"No. And I hadn't come to stand around getting wet, either."

"Just answer the question," he snapped, transferring his hands to his hips and planting his feet apart. Well *really*, I thought, if throwing your weight around were an Olympic sport, this kid would be in line for a gold medal.

"As a matter of fact, I'd been chatting with Nigel Aitken," I answered calmly, adding: "His uncle was an old family friend." This, I felt, gave us a kind of status. Besides, the fact that Aitken-Sneath was dead made it unlikely that our inquisitor would find out it wasn't true.

Far from behaving as though he suspected a lie, however, the boy became almost ingratiating.

"Oh...so you came here often, did you?"

I wobbled my head, Indian style. "Now and then, now and then."

He relinquished the hands on hips pose and moved a step closer. He was trying to seem friendly, I think.

"Well, I don't suppose old what's his name - "

"Aitken-Sneath," put in the younger brother.

"Yes, I don't suppose old Aitken-Sneath ever mentioned a sort of a...how shall I put it?"

"A secret compartment," suggested the younger brother.

"Yes, a secret compartment. Or something like that. It could have been something he'd had made just before he died."

I paused before replying. If I said yes, but didn't say anymore, it could well make them start to suspect us again. It might make them wonder if we weren't looking for that compartment ourselves. Of course, I could have tried to send them off on a wild goose chase by saying, "Yes, I think Aitken-Sneath said something about hiding his treasures beneath the sitting room." But beneath the sitting room, or wherever else I chose, might be just where the hiding place was. So, all things considered, to pretend to complete ignorance seemed best.

Besides, at the back of my mind was the fear that Mandeville senior might pop up at any minute and see who we were.

"No, I can't recall that he did. But then, if it was secret, he wouldn't have, would he?" I replied at last.

They both seemed to see the sense in this.

"Anyway, we'd better be going. Our rackets will be getting wet," I added.

They seemed to see the sense in this too, surprisingly, for they began to nod and mutter: "Yes, yes, of course, of course." I was a trifle worried that in their newfound chumminess they might escort us from the grounds, and in so doing discover (a) that there weren't any rackets, and (b) that the fence had only just been cut; but at this point a window was thrown up in the house behind us and Mandeville shouted out: "Dickon! Rich!"

"Oh...we'd better go. Come on, Rich," said the elder boy. "You can see your own way out, I suppose..."

Yes, we could, we replied, and hardly had they turned back towards the house than we were in the shelter of the rhododendrons.

The question was, had Mandeville seen us, and, if so, had he recognised us? Now that we were protected by the bushes, I risked looking round and up at the house. A window on the first floor was open and a man was gazing out in our direction. He appeared to be squinting. It was Mandeville, of course, and the main impression I had was that he was puzzled. He must have been wondering what two youths were doing in his garden, but it didn't look to me as though he had spotted that we weren't just any youths - we were Waterman youths. Probably Clara's red head had thrown him off the scent - for when he'd seen her last she hadn't yet dyed her hair. At any rate, he wasn't shouting at us, or showing any signs of frenzy, or reaching for his mobile to call the police.

I let out a sigh of relief, and we returned through the box grove to the fence. We'd got away with it.

Developments

However, we hadn't found the manuscript, nor did it seem very likely that we would. That, I realised - once I'd finished congratulating myself on our good fortune in evading not only Mandeville himself but also his dreadful sons' inquisition - was the long and short of it.

Mandeville was now entrenched in *The Junipers* and, as Dickon's questions had suggested, the finding of the secret compartment and the manuscript within it was very much on his mind. And on his sons' minds, too. From the chit-chat on the occasion of Mandeville's visit to our house I'd gathered that his sons did not live with him but with their mother. The fact that they were here with him now meant, presumably, that they had been brought in to help him in his hunt. And with three full time searchers on the job, it couldn't be long before *The Junipers* yielded up its secret.

That this would be the probable outcome was given added emphasis by the news which broke the next morning. Dad heard it on the radio while doing some early morning washing up, and relayed it to the rest of us as we stumbled into breakfast.

The gist of it was that Quine's project was now out in the open. Somehow the news had been leaked to the *Sunday Times* and its reporters had done a big article on the affair. Moreover, since Quine's Ronnie design was considered 'controversial', the article had been deemed worthy of a mention on the radio.

As a rule, we didn't get a Sunday paper - Dad couldn't stand them at any price - but this time he made an exception and went out and bought one as soon as the shops were open. We read the article grimly: Dad first, then Mum, then myself, and Clara last of all.

I won't bore you with the details or the potted biography of Quine, who came across as a kind of post-modern superhero - there was a big picture of his chunky head above the caption: IS THIS THE MOST CREATIVE MIND IN BRITAIN? - and as for the facts, we knew them already. No, it was the editorial slant that really mattered, and here - after weighing up the potential argument between those who were described as 'the Conservationists' on the one hand and those who were described as 'the Visionaries' on the other, the paper came down squarely on the side of the latter. The reporters reasoned that while certain sections of the community were bound to be outraged at the prospect of a giant pop star being carved into the Surrey landscape, such outrage was the very stuff of modern art and, if anything, should be encouraged. Indeed, Sohrab Quine was to be congratulated for his courage and astonishing creativity, etc. Plus it was high time that iconic Youth Culture figures like Ronnie Bastard, who were known and admired the world over and who brought in tankfuls of dosh for the Exchequer, were recognised as being an essential part of our heritage and got the respect they deserved.

"Well," pronounced Dad sadly after he had read the article a second time, "If this is the line the National Trust takes, there's no hope for us."

Things didn't look much better at lunchtime, when the news of the Chalk Figure project was aired on TV. First, we heard the facts themselves. Then we were treated to a sample of public opinion. The news team had gone out into the streets of Reigate and asked a few of the locals what they thought of the idea of a gigantic Ronnie on the hill above the town. "Ronnie Bastard? Well, why not?", "Oh, I don't think I should like that...no, I don't think I should like that at all," and "What? Ronnie Bastard on Woodcote Hill? Yeah, great idea. Brilliant," were some of the replies. This was followed by an interview with Quine himself. We saw him lounging on a leopard skin bean bag in what I took to be his arty flat, one arm round the Blonde and his head looking chunkier than ever.

"How did you get the idea of doing this chalk figure in the first place?" the reporter asked.

"It just came to me in a flash," answered Quine. "The Unconscious, y'know...who can say how it works?"

We also got to hear from a representative of the already-forming opposition to the scheme. The rep. in question wasn't some trendy environmentalist who might have served Dad's cause, however, but some old blinkered buffer from the Reigate and District Conservative Party who was about as unhip as you could get. Also, he acted like he didn't know who Ronnie Bastard was. Whether this was out of a misplaced sense of humour or because he genuinely hadn't a clue wasn't clear, but as a debating ploy it simply didn't work. After all, when The Complete Bastards had thrown a two-day bash at Knebworth the previous summer, close on two million people had applied for tickets. In other words, whatever else he was, Ronnie Bastard was certainly one well-known guy.

There could be little question, therefore, who had the better of this particular argument. The winner was Sohrab Quine with his humble artist routine.

And if there were any doubts about this, they were swept away by the P.M.'s off-the-cuff remarks transmitted on the early evening news. He was somewhere In the Middle East, trying to win the fish and chip shop franchise for Britain, I think, when the question was put to him: what did he think of the Ronnie Bastard chalk giant idea? He must have been briefed already, for he came back as quick as one of Quine's flashes with:

"I think it's a splendid idea, splendid. Ronald Bastard has worked wonders for Great Britain P.L.C. and it's quite right that he should be honoured in this way."

In addition, the Chairman of the Arts Council was quoted as saying that "the people of Surrey will learn to love" their new chalk giant. Even the Prince of Wales was said to have described the plan as "funky".

"Worse and worse," said Dad as he switched the *News* off with an irritable flourish of his handset. And indeed, it was hard to see how anything could stop this juggernaut of political luminaries and Art World top bods from trundling over Dad's dream. The go-ahead for Quine's chalk giant looked like a dead cert.

For my part, I wondered how Mandeville was taking this. He would surely have heard the news by now - and knowing that in less than two weeks' time the fate of the Shiva figure would be sealed, he'd be bound to be searching for the Bastable book with even greater zeal.

Of course, it was one of the ironies of the affair that it was as much in his interest to find the manuscript and preserve the chalk giant image as it was in ours. Though I don't know which I feared the more: the destruction of the Shiva carving, or Mandeville's finding the proof of its existence and taking all the credit.

At any rate, curiosity made me want to find out how Mandeville was progressing. I didn't quite know how I was going to do this, but another visit to *The Junipers* seemed the best bet. We might re-encounter our pals of yesterday there, and I had a feeling that if we did, it would be easy to tell from their manner whether or not their search had been successful.

If it hadn't been successful, it meant that we were still in with the slimmest of chances. And if it *had* been successful - well, Clara's argument that the Bastable book was of too late a date to contain the necessary proof of the Shiva figure in itself still held. The manuscript probably pointed to something else - though I couldn't guess what. Another, much earlier book, perhaps. But at least this suggested that the finding of the manuscript would not be the end of the trail; and therefore, once again, we would still be in with a chance - though the odds of our beating Bryan Mandeville to the post were getting longer by the minute.

I put these points to Clara and she agreed with my analysis. She tried to give the impression that she didn't really care what happened, and said outright that as far as she could see there wasn't the slightest hope of reviving Dad's career. All the same, I felt that her mud-pack of coolness was breaking up and that her old, expressive features were just about becoming visible again.

So, after an early dinner, we went up once more to *The Junipers*.

The Search Continued

It was a fine, warm evening and as we neared the house we saw a wavering line of smoke ascending, as though it had been painted on the cobalt blue sky with a Chinese brush.

"They must be having a bonfire," Clara remarked.

They were. The gates were open and the Mandeville boys were standing by a fire at one side of the gravel forecourt. One was swigging what looked to be fizzy water from a large green plastic bottle, the other was poking the fire with a stick and now and then throwing on papers from a pile beside him. The latter - who was the smaller, ginger-haired boy, the one called Rich - caught sight of us and whispered something to his brother. The brother put his bottle down, wiped his mouth with the back of his hand and gave us a stony, suspicious look. Then he wandered over. He had one of those rolling, dorky walks, like he was on the deck of a ship, and there was something about his unhurried progress across the drive that seemed to say he was not particularly pleased to see us.

"Want something?" he said, stopping a few yards away.

No, it wasn't the friendly greeting, or at least the courteous hello, that we might have expected. I wondered what had occasioned this return to their initial attitude towards us. Perhaps their father had cross-questioned them about the people to whom they'd been talking in the garden and had warned them against us. Or maybe their rudeness just came naturally.

"We wondered how you were getting on," I replied.

"Getting on what?"

"Well, settling in - you know."

"We've settled in."

There was a pause.

"And with your quest for the secret compartment," I added.

That was putting the cat among the pigeons all right, but his laconic answers had left me no choice.

He stepped forward a pace or two and folded his arms. His face had the unfinished look of a boy of seventeen, still replete with puppy fat, and it contrasted oddly with the gangster cool of his pose.

"Who told you we were looking for a secret compartment?" he demanded.

"Well, you did. More or less."

He chewed on this for a moment. "I may have mentioned a compartment. I didn't say we were looking for it."

It wasn't convincing, and I guess he knew it. Anyway, this was Clara's cue and she took it with admirable efficiency.

"Well, if *my* house contained a secret compartment, I'd certainly want to find it. In fact," she added, as though the thought had only just occurred to her and had not been discussed at length on our journey here, "We could help you look, if you like." In saying this, she adopted something of a little-girl voice and blushed becomingly.

I don't know if I've mentioned it, but Clara was actually quite a nice-looking girl - or would have been, if she hadn't tried to look like something found on a refuse heap and reanimated by a miracle of modern science. 'Fine-featured' is I think the term. At any rate, her statement worked a charm on young Dickon. He seemed to notice for the first time that Clara was a girl, and he responded with something approaching cordiality. Indeed, he seemed to crumple slightly and you could almost hear the sound of hot air escaping from his ego.

"Well, I don't know," he said, biting a thumb. "As it happens, we *are* looking for a sort of hiding place and we could certainly use some help...but I don't know what Dad would say. He wants to keep the whole thing under wraps until we've found it. But what I say is, our chances of finding it can only go up if we have some help."

"But of course," stated Clara, as though that was that.

Our plan, if you could call it that, had been (a) to check on the Mandeville's progress, and (b) to inveigle our way into the house and assist with the search ourselves, if possible. Actually, the chances of putting this second intention into practice had seemed pretty remote, but all of a sudden I could see our way to doing it. And if *we* should be the ones who found the hiding place - well, it might be possible to smuggle the manuscript out of the house, or to borrow the relevant passage at least. Anyway - in for a penny, in for a pound.

"Is your father not in, then?" I asked, to be sure of our ground. The first thing I'd noticed had been that the garage doors were open and that the Range Rover had gone, which, taken together with the way Dickon was talking, implied that Mandeville was indeed out - but it was best to be certain. Of course, if we were invited in and Mandeville found us there, it was highly likely that he'd promptly send us packing. Yet he couldn't be aware that we knew about the Bastable, and - you never knew - it might even amuse him to use our help.

"No. He's gone back to our other house to get a torch."

"You mean, you have *two* houses?" queried Clara, looking up at the Victorian bulk of *The Junipers* with an amazed expression. I hoped she wasn't overdoing it.

Dickon answered with a rueful grin taken straight from the Quine *Book of Looks*.

"Well, yeah...as a matter of fact we do. Anyway, you might as well come in. But you haven't told me your name..."

This last was addressed to my sister. In my own name he seemed to have no interest.

"Clara."

"That's nice. I'm Dickon."

"So, Dickon, where have you looked for this secret compartment, or whatever it is?" Clara asked, getting down to brass tacks.

"Pretty much everywhere, except in the cellar and attic. That's why my father's gone to get a torch. There aren't any lights in the attic."

We were on the steps of the porch now and about to enter the house. Suddenly, however, the younger brother darted over and asked what we were doing. Dickon told him we were going to help in the search for the hiding place. Rich responded with: "What? Are you mad? Dad'll be furious if he finds any strangers in the house." (He laid particular emphasis on the word *strangers*, glaring the while at Clara's neo-punk hair.) But Dickon replied with what amounted to a proprietary air that Clara wasn't a stranger, she was Clara.

"Besides," he added, "If we find the compartment while he's out, Dad'll be really pleased. Remember what he said about bonus points." He turned to us and explained: "Dad has a system. It's a bit like air miles. You get points for the good things you do, and eventually they pay out in computer games or restaurant meals, things like that."

"I still don't like it," said Rich.

"Oh, shut up, Rich. You just get on with burning the old man's stuff and leave the hunting to me," said Dickon. "We bought the house with most of its contents and all the last owner's papers. Dad's been going through them and chucking out what we don't need," he explained.

Rich restated his opinion that going against their Dad's express orders was a bad idea. "And you won't get any bonus points, you'll lose all the points you've got now."

"Oh, calm down, Rich," said Dickon.

"Yes, calm down, Tich - I mean Rich," said Clara. "I don't expect we'll find anything, anyway."

"Yeah, well, there probably isn't anything *to* be found," Rich responded darkly. "If you ask me, old Aitken-Sneath was crazy and the whole thing's a wild goose chase."

"Maybe, maybe not," said Dickon. "But you'd better watch those papers - the wind's blowing them away."

Dickon was right. A wind had got up and was beginning to scatter the topmost sheets of paper from the pile beside the fire. Perhaps they were the ones that had been in the filing cabinet through which I'd looked yesterday, I thought. Mandeville must have been checking through them for clues as to the manuscript's whereabouts, or to the nature of its contents.

At any rate, while Rich was distracted we went into the house and through to the stairwell. The sitting room door was wide open, and as we began to climb the stairs we could see that the carpet had been rolled back and the suite of chairs turned upside down. A glimpse into the anteroom which led into the conservatory showed that that had been ransacked, too.

"You must want to find this secret place an awful lot," I remarked.

"Yes...what's in it, anyway?" asked Clara.

Dickon paused at the top of the stairs. You could see that while he was anxious to please, the question was not a welcome one.

"Oh...just an old book of some sort. Actually, there may be lots of things there, but it's the book my Dad wants."

"What kind of book?" said Clara, wide-eyed.

"Well..." Dickon wriggled a bit, but her ingénue directness was hard to evade. "Oh, I might as well tell you the whole story, I suppose." He moved on a few paces and showed us into the study. "Here, this is one of the most likely places. It was the late owner's study - though I dare say you know that already, if you were pals of his. Now, if we can shift the furniture over there, we can get the carpet up and check the flooring."

We started moving the desk and cabinets into one corner while the boy went on talking.

"It all started when some colleague of my father's - *ex*-colleague, I should say - imagined he saw a figure of some Indian god cut into the hillside behind this house. It sounds really off the wall, I know, but Dad had the intelligence to see that there just might be something in it.

"Now, the guy who had the idea in the first place, who saw this image or dreamed that he saw it, or whatever it was - he was some kind of loser, according to Dad. He didn't know the first thing about research, he couldn't find any evidence to substantiate his claims, he rubbed everyone up the wrong way, he just wasn't up to it and in the end he lost his job. Exit him from the story.

"But Dad had more persistence. He did some investigating himself and found out that the guy who used to live here, Aitken-Sneath, was a local historian. He got pally with him, and pretty soon Aitken-Sneath let on that he'd discovered some sort of proof that this Chalk Giant really had existed. Dad was really excited - I mean, *really* excited - but before he could do a deal with Aitken-Sneath, the silly old fool went and died.

"However, he'd told Dad that the proof was in some old book of which he had the only copy, and that he'd taken good care to hide it. So that's what we're doing - we're looking for the hiding place."

Inwardly, I congratulated myself - and Clara, too - for resisting the impulse to hit him with the table lamp. Indeed, so thoroughly had Clara thrown herself into the part that she managed to say, with a chirpy wonderment:

"Gosh, do you mean to say that your father bought this whole place just so he could get his hands on that book?"

"That's right. But remember, it's not any old book. The finding of it could crown Dad's career."

"He must be very determined."

"He is," agreed Dickon. "I'm the same."

I examined the study's parquet flooring, all of which seemed to be intact, while Dickon took the drawers out of the desk and peered and tapped inside the remaining wooden skeleton in search of hidden cubby-holes.

It occurred to me that some logical thinking was in order, and after a minute or two of the same I concluded that underneath the floorboards was a very unlikely place for Aitken-Sneath to have hidden the manuscript. You had to bear in mind that he'd been an old man with not long to go when he'd had this hiding place made (*if* he had had it made), and somehow I couldn't see him shifting furniture about and rolling carpets back whenever he wanted to dip into his Bastable. And if that was so, it also ruled out the attic. He wouldn't have wanted to clamber up there at his advanced age and in his condition - for I imagined that it required a certain amount of clambering, if there was no electric light supplied. Besides, his character as revealed in his letter had struck me as rather too precious for such activities. And crafty, too. Which, on reflection, ruled out the obvious places - like the study, or his bedroom, or the cellar. No, he would have hidden the manuscript in a place which was at once *unlikely* and *accessible*.

That was the gist of my thoughts, and I was just running through them again, checking the reasoning - when there was the distinct, and in this case distinctly unpleasant, sound of a car pulling into the drive on the far side of the house at considerable speed and slewing to a halt.

The Dismissal

"Well, there doesn't seem to be anything here. Perhaps we'd better go now," I said casually.

Dickon took another leaf out of Sohrab Quine's book and ignored me again.

"That should be Dad with the torch. We can check the attic together. It covers the whole of the top of the house, so it'll be a big job," he remarked to Clara.

"All the same, I think we should be going," I repeated, taking hold of Clara's arm.

She seemed reluctant to speak, as though she couldn't quite decide what pattern of behaviour her character would follow. Dickon started to say why didn't I go, then, and Clara could stay and help out - his father would be delighted. But already I'd heard the front door slam, and the next moment there were thunderous footsteps on the stairs.

"Dickon! Dickon!" roared a voice.

"Yes, Dad?"

Mandeville appeared on the landing, his domed forehead glowing and his small eyes flashing. The top two buttons of his shirt were undone and I noticed that, in spite of the heat, he still had his gorilla hide underwear on. "Just what is going on here?" he demanded.

"I've got some help, Dad. I've got - " began the wretched Dickon, deflating by the second. He didn't finish.

"I thought I made my instructions perfectly clear!" Mandeville turned to us. "I'm sorry to say that this house is not yet - how shall I put it? - *open to the public.* So, perhaps if you'll just..." He stopped and peered at Clara, then turned and stared at me.

Suddenly I saw that, though sane by the standards of the world and undeniably not lacking in authority, Bryan Mandeville had pretty well become unhinged. He was sweating, he clutched the torch in his hand as though it was a weapon, his eyes were those of a fanatic in a hurry. It may have been the news of Quine's project that had triggered this attack, though I imagined that it must have been coming on for awhile. As though I were a computer onto which was being copied the contents of a floppy disk, I seemed to perceive all at once the ambition which drove him; the frustration he'd felt in having no scope, as an academic in an obscure field, for that ambition to realise itself; the jealousy from which he must have suffered when my father discovered the Shiva image; and his absolute determination to be the first to prove that the figure did exist: I saw it all. It must have seemed to him that things were playing into his hands when first Aitken-Sneath had talked about finding some evidence, and then when he'd been left the money with which to buy this house...but now, you could see, his faith in himself and his luck was slipping. It was slipping fast. He'd spent a fortune, he'd got the house, yet he still hadn't got the manuscript and, moreover, time was running out. I almost felt sorry for him - but not quite. In any case, he didn't give me the chance.

With a rapid twist of his head he looked back at his son. "Don't you know who these children are?"

"Well, sure. This is - "

"They're Edmund Waterman's children."

Dickon looked blankly at his father.

"You know - the loser," said Clara.

The flabby balloon that was Dickon Mandeville deflated further. His father, meanwhile, was going red and white alternately. In fact, he looked as though he were trying to impersonate a belisha beacon. Nevertheless, he mastered himself sufficiently to be able to say to us with a certain calm terseness:

"I don't know what far-fetched story you told my son, but I'll thank you to be going. I have a great deal of work to do. My son will show you out."

And so, for the second time in two days we left *The Junipers* at speed - and for the second time we left without the object for which we'd come.

The Bill

While this unfortunate turn of events didn't do much for Clara's and my morale, it couldn't have been a whole lot of fun for Dickon either. But as for Rich, whom we passed in the driveway: he seemed ecstatic.

"What did I tell you? What did I *tell* you?" he inquired of his brother, half-excitedly, half-mockingly.

"All right, all right," Dickon responded moodily.

For our part we said nothing, and indeed, there seemed nothing to say. Wordlessly, he saw us out of the gates, pushed them to behind us with a *clang* of finality, and wandered back to join his brother.

I signalled to Clara that we should stay out of sight behind the gate pier for a moment and listen to the brothers' exchanges. Maybe we would be able to gather more information.

Except for a "Wha-a-at?" and a "Waterman's kids? You're joking!" from Rich, however, it was hard to make out what they were saying. Meanwhile, black and half-burnt bits of paper blew over the wall and settled on the grass verge beside us. The sound of voices ceased altogether and there was a slight, stealthy, rustling noise. Too late, I recognised the sound of footsteps on gravel, and the next moment Rich's face appeared a foot or two from mine, with just the wrought iron gate between us.

"I *thought* so! Would you believe it? They're still here, *eavesdropping*," he crowed to his brother. It was bad enough being called a 'kid' - a word I've always detested - by someone younger and smaller than myself, but this was too much. "Go on - get out of it!" he shouted, his freckled face puckering up into a snarl.

"This is public property," I began to argue, but Clara pulled me away.

"Come on, Dan, we don't need this..."

She was right, of course. I began to follow her, when another of the half-burnt leaves of paper from the bonfire drifted over the wall - which must have acted as a windbreak - and fluttered down in front of me. It seemed to be asking to be caught, so I caught it.

It was an invoice of some description, singed down the left hand side but still readable. As we strolled at a dignified pace back down the lane, ignoring Rich's muted jeers, I noticed that it was dated May 10th, five weeks ago. The title at the top of the sheet read: *Crabbit & Sons, Stonemasons.*

"That's funny," I said. "It's dated five weeks ago. That can't be long before Aitken-Sneath wrote his letter."

"Let me have a look."

I passed it over to Clara. She stopped and read it, moving a finger over the words and numbers.

"That's odd."

"What's odd?"

"Well...it's just that I didn't notice that anything had been done to the stonework."

I was about to say, "Oh, really?" in a sceptical tone, when I recalled that Clara was quite a brainbox when it came to stone. Before getting into making constructions out of rusty metal, etc, she'd made something of a study of stone, and as a matter of fact the block from which she'd carved the dancing Shiva had come from Crabbit & Sons. Their yard was down on Babylon Lane, on the far side of the village.

"So, what are you saying?" I asked.

"Well, the description of the work's a bit cryptic, isn't it? Listen to this: 'Cutting out and making good'. That tells us nothing." She paused. "Unless it's that the whole business was sort of *clandestine*."

"You mean, it was to do with the secret compartment?"

"Exactly. I don't know about you, but I'd pictured Aitken-Sneath getting a carpenter in to do the work. But suppose he got a stonemason in instead. If you're right and the draft letter to Mandeville was written about a week before he died, then this work must have been done just a couple of weeks before he put pen to paper. And that would fit with when he must have had the compartment made. Assuming he *did* have it made."

I was excited yet unconvinced. "It's possible, I guess... But if we call on Crabbit and Sons and ask them what it was all about, will they tell us anything?"

"We can but see," said Clara.

Crabbit & Sons

The stonemason's yard in Babylon Lane had a shabby, run down look about it. Of course, there'd never been much call for stone-building in our county of greensand and chalk. You had to go west to find limestone, hence stone-built houses were rare in Surrey - and Crabbit & Sons could never have done a roaring trade. But now the piles of York stone paving slabs and upright polished granite and marble headstones in the yard conveyed a sad, funereal mood.

It was Monday afternoon. Skipping games, I'd come home early from school, and likewise Clara had left her art college after lunch. Time was of the essence and we had to interview Mr Crabbit before Bryan Mandeville found - or stumbled upon - the compartment. Naturally, we knew that the invoice we'd got hold of might have had nothing whatsoever to do with a secret hiding place for Aitken-Sneath's valuables, but it was the only lead we had and we both felt obliged to follow it up.

Passing a dilapidated shed, we came to the office. Of his sons there was no sign, but Mr Crabbit himself, his face and hair white with Bath stone dust, was on the phone. He was in his late fifties, I guessed, and by his looks was of a canny, taciturn disposition. But not too canny and not too taciturn, I hoped.

The question uppermost in our minds had been: how to approach him? One part of me had argued that we should make up some story - for example, that the new owner of *The Junipers* had sent us to ask Mr Crabbit, as Clara knew him slightly, whether he knew where the hiding place was; or that Aitken-Sneath's nephew, when tidying up, had come across the bill and was anxious to check that it had been paid. But the other part of me had taken the view that this was all too devious by half, and that, as ever, honesty was the best policy. Clara shared this latter view, so it was the one we adopted.

But before we could speak, Mr Crabbit spoke to us. Or to my sister, to be exact. Putting the phone down, he said:

"You're the lass who had that block of Hoptonwood, aren't you? That must have been all of two year ago. How did you get on with it?"

Clara must have been torn between the wish to be affable and a desire not to have to think about the unfinished sculpture, for her reply came out in a peculiar stop-start manner.

"Oh...quite well, yes. Yes, *quite* well, I suppose," etc.

"She made a really nice job of it," I put in. "Only she never quite finished it."

Mr Crabbit gave her a sharp glance. With the cream-coloured dust all over him, he looked as though he were in the middle of making up to play the part of Father Christmas in a chain store grotto.

"Perseverance is what you need, perseverance. You can't learn a craft like stone-carving overnight, but if you persevere, you'll get there in the end."

"Yes, of course," said Clara hastily. "Maybe I'll go back to it. But the reason we came here is because, well, we wondered if you could help us."

Encouraged by his receptive, listening air, she then went on to tell him the whole story, from my first sighting of the Chalk Giant to Dad's disastrous attempt to reveal it academically to Sohrab Quine's project to the possible clue contained in *The Junipers*. I couldn't help noticing that since the moment she had interpreted the stonemason's bill as being of importance, she'd become a lot more involved in our quest. In fact, she'd become more animated in general - and this was reflected in the way she told her story. She only paused once, to ask if she was taking up too much of Mr Crabbit's time.

He waved a dusty hand. "No, no, business is slack right now. Go on, go on," he said, gazing at her face with a penetrating, inscrutable look, as though he were going to carve it from memory.

And so she went on, or rather off to the side, detailing Mandeville's machinations and the finding of the invoice, and then coming back to the point - which was that we needed to know, if such a thing were permissible, what exactly was the work he'd done for Aitken-Sneath.

"Well, why didn't you say so? It's true that it was an unusual job, and old Mr Aitken-Sneath did try to get me to keep my mouth shut about it - though who he thought I was going to tell, I don't know. Anyway, he's passed on now, so I don't suppose it matters *what* I say." This was said with what I took to be a trace of a wink. "No, I don't suppose it matters very much if I let the odd fact slip out. And if, as you say, the house belongs to this Mr Mandeville now - well, whatever I say won't be of much use to *you*." Here I thought I detected another rapid movement of a white-flecked eyelid. "Though it wasn't in the house, exactly - what Mr Aitken-Sneath wanted me to do. It was in the conservatory."

"The grotto!" I exclaimed.

Maybe it was the image of Mr Crabbit as Santa Claus that had put the word into my head, but it all seemed suddenly obvious. The conservatory was on the ground floor, right next to the anteroom which, by the look of it, had been in constant use. The grotto had been near at hand, yet no-one would have thought of looking there for a secret compartment. Of course, there was the danger of its contents getting wet - but the conservatory roof had probably been intact when Aitken-Sneath had had the compartment made.

"Exactly. The grotto. He wanted me to cut a segment off the side, then hollow out a space within and line it with lead, then replace the outer segment. That was the difficult bit: to attach the segment so that it could be opened neatly, yet so that the joins were watertight and more or less invisible. In the end I put hinges on it, so that it swings upwards. I wouldn't say it's completely invisible, though...still, you'd have to know it was there, if you wanted to see it. And Mr Aitken-Sneath did his best to cover it up with ferns and suchlike. Said it was to be a sort of private cubby-hole. I wonder if you could find it...but then, you're not going to look, are you?"

His resemblance to Father Christmas had increased markedly during the course of this explanation, but now, I felt, he'd handed out all his presents and his sack was empty. He wasn't going to say anymore, and it was up to us to make use of his information - if we dared.

"Now, I'd best be getting on with things..." he said.

"Yes, of course."

We thanked him profusely, and left.

The Raid

"Tonight," I said as we walked back down Babylon Lane, "It's got to be tonight."

"It'll be a big risk."

"Yes, but we can't afford to hang about."

"Maybe we could lure Mandeville away and go this evening. A telephone call mentioning the manuscript and summoning him to...I don't know...Brighton or Tunbridge Wells or London, might do the trick," Clara reasoned.

"But it wouldn't lure his two wretched sons away, and there's no guarantee that an egghead like Mandeville would fall for it, either. He'd probably want more information than we could give, and then stay at home and lay a trap and catch us red-handed. And *that's* a fate too awful to be contemplated."

"Yes - and then he'd probably guess that we knew something and only let us go if we told him what it was," said Clara. "Okay - tonight. But *late* tonight. The mood he was in yesterday, he'll probably be up half the night turning the place upside down."

"All right. We'll plan to get there at two in the morning. Even Mandeville must sleep sometime. And I hope it's not one of Dad's sleepless nights, either," I replied.

It was lucky that the bedrooms in our house were so distant from one another: mine at the back of the house, Mum's and Dad's at the front and on the other side, and

Clara's upstairs. This meant that when my alarm clock went off at half-past one in the morning, it couldn't be heard by my parents, and the same with my sister's. To be on the safe side, I'd muffled the alarm by putting a pillow on top of the clock - though as it turned out, I need hardly have bothered, because at half-past one I was still wide awake. I hadn't been able to sleep a wink for thinking of what might happen if (a) or if (b) or if (c), etc.

Clara, on the other hand, had slept like a log until the alarm woke her up. She was a surprising girl in some ways.

We rendezvoused in the dining room and left by the back door. For once, Clara's coal-black clobber was just what was needed. I wore a pair of jeans, a dark blue sweater, and gloves. I carried a torch - and the wire cutters too, in case Mandeville had discovered the break in the fence and mended it.

One other thing: I'd left a note on my bed reading, "Back soon. Don't worry."

As our eyes grew accustomed to the darkness, the moonlit night began to seem astonishingly bright. You may know that old riddle beloved of scientists: why, when the sky's full of millions of stars, isn't the night sky as bright as day? Well, I was beginning to think, "What's the problem? It *is* as bright as day," when I walked into our gate post.

This sobered me up.

We walked past the Lindenmeyer's cottage at the foot of our drive, then on by the path through the bracken to where it joined the lane to Woodcote Hill. The few houses we passed were silent and secretive-seeming, their windows dark with mystery. Swift-moving clouds came and went across the half moon's face. I was anxious that we shouldn't be seen by any passing motorists, but no cars drove by. So far as I could tell, we reached *The Junipers* unobserved.

"I'm beginning to feel that I've spent half my life here," whispered Clara.

"Yeah, I know what you mean."

As we'd anticipated, the gates were securely locked. Moreover, a light - which presumably dated from Aitken-Sneath's time - shone out above the porch. We went past the house and turned down the narrow path to the hill. The cuts in the fence had not been repaired. We climbed through.

"Now for the tricky bit," I whispered.

We inched our way between the box trees and into the rhododendrons. The slightest noises sounded magnified. I was excited and scared in more or less equal measure.

That is, until we looked out onto the terrace across the lawn. Then my excitement dwindled and my fear increased. For a moment I wondered if Mandeville wasn't lurking in the sitting room, having guessed by some occult inspiration that we would attempt to burgle his house tonight. As I stared at the windows, things seemed to move and take shape behind them...but this, I told myself, was just an effect of the darkness, and there was nobody there - the residents were asleep.

Then I wondered if it was really worth it: to go ahead with this escapade. What if the manuscript wasn't there?

Or what if it was there, and we took it, but it didn't prove anything? Would it really matter if the hill with its enigmatic design of Shiva dancing - a design which for hundreds of years no-one had known existed - was disfigured by a giant white Ronnie Bastard? Who really cared?

I thought of my father. He cared. But even more than that, I cared myself. It had nothing to do with the age of the thing. It had nothing to do with its archaeological significance. It had nothing to do with its newsworthiness. Nor did I care that much about the past - in which, as Sohrab Quine had astutely pointed out, we could no longer live. It was the poetry of the image that moved me. That, and its meaning. That the land, our land, held a deeper purpose than to be a backdrop for the faithless to stamp their logos on.

So, after having watched the dark, still house for four or five minutes and seen nothing to deter us, we set off across the lawn. I hadn't gone more than a couple of paces, however, when Clara clutched my arm. For an instant I thought that someone must be watching us. But she only whispered, *"For goodness sake look where you're going,"* and I glanced down.

I had almost stepped into the lily pond, the one with the green slime on top.

Breathing a sigh of relief, I followed in her footsteps across the lawn. We climbed onto the terrace and arrived at the conservatory. The broken pane of glass was still missing - since, as I'd suspected, Mandeville had not had time to get it mended, even if he'd noticed it. Clara went through the hole and I followed.

Only somehow I managed to put my foot on a fragment of broken glass as I did so.

It scrunched beneath my weight and the noise seemed to echo round the room. Clara looked daggers at me - or at least, I felt that she did, for it was too dark to see any facial details. The moon was hidden again, and in any case it was darker in this glass room than it was outside in the open air.

Though the sound of my foot on the broken glass appeared loud to us, however, it couldn't have travelled very far; no lights went on and no-one came to investigate. In fact, I began to wonder whether the Mandevilles might not have gone back to their house in Epsom for the night...

Carefully skirting the half-empty pool, we went over to the grotto. My feeling, which I'd mentioned to Clara, was that the hidden cubby-hole would be on the side nearest to the door into the house. To Aitken-Sneath, that would have been the most convenient place. So it was there that we began to feel for an upward-swinging 'lid' of stone. I doubted that there'd be a lock or catch - the weight of the stone itself would serve to seal the lid, once closed.

The moon came out again, obviating the need for the torch, though making us feel the more exposed.

And then Clara found it. Brushing a fern aside, she took hold of a knobbly protrusion of stone and pulled it upwards. It lifted easily, revealing a space about two feet wide by eighteen inches high and presumably fairly deep.

It was, as Mr Crabbit had told us, lined with lead, and it contained a wooden box. While Clara held the stone lid up, I took the box out. I put it on the tiled floor. It wasn't locked, and very gently I opened it.

There was only one thing inside: a book with what felt like a worn calfskin cover. There were no other valuables. In his letter, Aitken-Sneath had mentioned hiding them along with the book, but either he'd changed his mind or he'd not got round to it.

I took the book out, shut the box and replaced it. Clara closed the stone lid and the fern fell back into place - as Mr Crabbit had said, it must have been planted in one of the grotto's natural sockets deliberately, in order to hide the rectangular cut around the lid from view. Then we were ready to leave the conservatory.

It was as simple as that.

Correction. It was *almost* as simple as that...

The Fox

I felt triumphant. Incredibly, we'd succeeded. We had the book. We'd beaten Mandeville to it. But at the same time I knew very well that this was the most dangerous moment of the whole operation. If Mandeville found us now, we'd be caught red-handed. Not only that, but we wouldn't have anything to bargain with either. We couldn't say, "Look, we can help you find what you're looking for, if you'll only let us go," since we already had it on us. And we couldn't hide it, either - it was just too big.

No, he would simply take the book off us and, unless I'd misread his character completely, call the cops.

At this point, I suddenly remembered that I still had the back door key in my pocket from when we'd first searched the house. I went over and tried the door. So far as I could tell, it was bolted on the inside but not locked - unsurprisingly, since I had the key. I swiftly locked it and put the key back in my pocket.

If anyone did spot us and try to follow us, *that* would delay them a little, I told myself with a grim smile.

Then I turned to follow Clara, who was already half-way through the hole in the conservatory's glass wall. I passed her the book - she was outside now - and raised my leg in order to get through the wall myself.

But then - I'm not quite sure how - the torch, which had been stuffed in my pocket, fell out. It was a heavy, metal torch of Dad's, virtually an antique, and it hit a part of the broken sheet of glass with a ringing crash. I suppose the sheet of glass must have been propped up on another piece of glass or a stone - but whatever the case, the resulting noise was a long way from the subtle crunch I'd made earlier with my foot. In the encompassing quietness of the windless garden, it sounded loud enough to wake the dead.

At any rate, it woke someone within the house, for an upstairs light went on. You could tell by the faint white rectangle which suddenly appeared on the lawn. I grabbed the torch, forced my way through where the broken pane had been, and ran across the terrace. Clara was lying on the grass below the balustrade, to the side of the white rectangle and just out of sight of the upstairs windows. With a leap, I joined her.

"Sorry. The torch - "

"*Shhh!*"

The light on the lawn became stronger, presumably because the bedroom curtain had been drawn back. I tried to reconstruct what must have happened. A quick upward glance told me that the light was on in Aitken-Sneath's old bedroom. Now, the likelihood was that Mandeville himself had taken that room. And having been awoken by the noise of the breaking glass, he must have switched on the bedside light, crossed to the window, opened the curtains - and was now peering out. I held my breath.

Then I turned my head and looked back across the lawn. Our trail was clearly visible in the thick grass and it led only one way: to the house! The grass was so thick that you couldn't actually see any footprints, and I guessed that it could have looked as though an animal had made the trail. But you could tell from the way the grass blades were bent that the trail led to the house, and that whoever had come by that route hadn't yet left by it. They might have left by a different route, of course, but if I'd been Mandeville, I'd have assumed they were still in the offing.

And if I'd been Mandeville and I'd heard that noise and seen that trail, so obviously made in the recent past, I would have surfed through my mental file of suspicious characters and in approximately half a second flat would have come up with the names: Dan and Clara Waterman.

Earlier, I mentioned that I had often passed the time reading Prisoner of War stories, of which Dad had a small collection. Now all at once the title of one of them came into my head:

Escape - or Die!

That just about summed it up, I felt.

"What do we do?" I whispered.

"Work our way round, then run for it..."

The probability was that Mandeville would run downstairs and come out into the garden. Or he might check the downstairs rooms first, in case we'd entered his house. Which would mean that while he was occupied in doing this, we should be able to run across the lawn unobserved. But we couldn't raise our heads and glance again at his bedroom window, for fear that he was still up there, looking out. Or that he'd woken and posted one of his sons there, while he went downstairs. Therefore the direct route across the lawn was out; we had, as Clara said, to work our way round beneath the balustrade until we came to the shrubbery beyond the conservatory. Once there, we'd be able to move under cover of the ornamental trees and hydrangea bushes to the shelter of the rhododendrons.

We'd hardly begun the journey, however, when we heard the back door's bolt being slipped back. Mandeville was there already. The door was shaken. He couldn't open it. It was shaken again, then released. My locking the door had done the trick. But only temporarily, of course. I thought: "He'll have gone to the sitting room windows: he'll be opening one of them..."

But by now we had reached the shrubbery and, keeping our heads down and carefully negotiating the stagnant lily pond, we made it safely to the rhododendrons. I risked a glance back. The nearest sash window in the sitting room had just been thrown up and Mandeville was stepping out onto the terrace - the window nearly touched the ground.

Once outside, he stood still, irresolutely looking around. After you've been in a bright room, it takes awhile for your eyes to adjust to the darkness and I doubted whether he could see much. Besides, he had no torch. And on top of that, he was hardly dressed for a chase through the undergrowth, since he was wearing only his pyjamas. And his gorilla suit underwear, of course.

I won't say I began to relax, but at least my nerves stopped snapping one after the other - *ping! ping! ping!* - like that.

By now, Mandeville was pacing up and down the terrace for a moment or two, as though to say to anyone who might be watching, "I'm here and I'm dangerous." Then he stopped by the conservatory. I guessed that he was staring through the glass at the door I'd locked - and apart from actually scratching his head, he gave every indication of being one puzzled man.

"How the hell did that door lock itself?" he must have been thinking. Then his mood seemed to change. Perhaps he caught sight of the pane of glass I'd broken or perhaps he simply felt annoyed at being woken up in the middle of the night, but clearly he decided to go on the offensive. Adopting a stealthy, crouching posture - which, incidentally, made him look more like a balding gorilla than ever - he came down onto the terrace and started following our trail across the lawn. Every few paces he would stop, listen, look to right and left, and then proceed on his way again. The moon was shining brightly, and by the time he reached the first of the ornamental trees my nerves were starting to *ping!* away again. He was getting dangerously close to where we were hiding, yet if we tried to get away now, we were bound to make a noise - and then he'd be bound to get a glimpse of us - and then, even if he didn't actually catch us, he'd be bound to guess who we were.

But just as he turned towards the rhododendrons, something miraculous happened. At a quick, trotting pace, a fox emerged from the shrubbery and crossed the lawn at right-angles to our trail. Mandeville paused and watched it, and as he did so you could almost hear his brain working.

Click click click - the broken pane of glass - *click click click* - the trail in the grass - *click click click* - the fox - *click click click* - the fox must have made the trail in the grass and broken the pane of glass - *click click click* - what a clever guy I am. He shrugged, straightened up, dropped the gorilla posture, and started walking back to the house.

And then he fell into the lily pond.

I don't think it was actually that deep, but he managed to fall onto his face in it, thus covering himself completely in weeds, leaves, algae, and rich black mud. Of course, he made a tremendous splash, too, and this - together with the burst of loud, colourful language that he used as he slithered up out of the pond, slipped back in, and hauled himself out again - seemed to wake his two sons. At any rate, another light went on in the house, and then another light.

Mandeville squelched back towards them, looking like the Creature from the Black Lagoon.

And with a nervous, muffled sigh of relief, Clara and I set off for home.

Bastable

So, who was Bastable? He turned out to be a puritan who, during Cromwell's Commonwealth, had taken it upon himself to oversee the destruction of what he saw as idol worship in the southern Home Counties. Sober-minded to a fault and lacking even a trace of an aesthetic sensibility, his *Journal Of The Year 1644* (for such was the title of his manuscript) recorded his travels through Western Kent and Surrey, stopping off at every church and wayside shrine in order to ensure that all 'heathen fripperies', 'glass gewgaws' and 'sacrilegious images' were burnt or smashed, removed or plastered over. In many places his work had already been done for him by the local hotheads, vandals and loonies, but here and there "I saw to it that ye glass in ye east window was broken up," or "I arranged for these appurtenances of Beelzebub to be destroyed", etc., etc.

It made for dispiriting reading - but I didn't have to wade through it all, for Aitken-Sneath had kindly marked the significant passage with a leather bookmark bought at Hampton Court.

The passage in question detailed a visit that Bastable had made to St Martha's Church at Hookland, just below Woodcote Hill, on October 20th, 1644. Apparently, this church had contained a number of wall-paintings "from the time of the Goths". In other words, from three or four hundred years before Bastable's time - or from even earlier, as his grasp of art history seemed somewhat limited. And in one of these murals, which showed scenes from the Old and New Testaments, a "curious figure cut into ye white chalke of ye hill above ye Church was depicted, a gigantic dancing man within a fiery, turning wheel", with, in the foreground, Adam and Eve relaxing among the apple trees. "Of this strange man nothing can now be seen," Bastable went on, "But many curious legends have grown up around this hill and this man, and I think it better for ye good health of our religion that this painting on ye north wall be covered up. I have ordered it to be washed with lime."

"That must mean 'whitewashed'," Clara remarked after she'd read it through for the second time.

It was early on Tuesday morning. We'd got back to the house unseen and gone back to our beds, deciding that the study of the manuscript would have to wait until we'd had some sleep. I'd kept the book in my room and, needless to say, hadn't even been able to slip into a doze. So I'd read the relevant passage - which had sent my mind into a whirl again. Around five, I'd drifted off for a couple of hours: it was now half-past seven, and we were in the sitting room.

"Well, let's hope it means 'whitewashed' and not 'washed off'. But the question is, what's there now?" I said.

"Bastable's reference itself must serve as some sort of proof," said Clara.

"Ye-e-es. But imagine if we could uncover the mural as well. Now, that *would* be a *coup*. Besides, there's one problem with Bastable as far as we're concerned..."

"What's that?"

"The part where we have to explain how it came into our possession."

"Yes, I see what you mean. We're the victims of our own success, kind of," said Clara. She mused for a moment. "Well, we could look in *Pevsner*. Dad's got a copy, and it would tell us something about the Church's interior."

"And whether it's still standing," I added.

"Oh, it's standing all right. You can see it from Woodcote Hill. You must have seen it hundreds of times, without knowing what it was."

So, we found the *Surrey* volume of Pevsner's *Buildings of England* - it was in the sitting room bookshelf - and looked up Hookland. St Martha's Church was listed, with the usual sniffy comments about its heavy-handed restoration and mediocre Victorian glass. Also, the glaring white-painted walls of the nave were described, together with an alabaster monument of a recumbent knight. But of the murals there was no mention.

"Well, we'd better go and look at it this evening," I said, "as soon as I get back from school."

In Hookland

When we got to Hookland, a mile or so from the foot of Woodcote Hill, we found the Church door open and a woman inside arranging flowers. The Church was small, consisting of the nave and chancel, the small flint tower with its pyramid roof, and a side chapel tacked onto the nave.

"Victorian work," said Clara confidently, looking at the latter.

"I wonder which wall's the north one," I said.

"Well, if the altar points east, then it must be this one," she reasoned, gesturing towards the wall on our left. At the near end (or, that's to say, the end away from the altar) a bucket was placed on the floor by the wall. Above it, in the plaster of the wall itself, an inch-wide crack ran six or seven feet down from the vaulted roof.

"Rain," said the lady who was doing the flowers.

"I beg your pardon?" I said.

"It's the rain that has made that crack," explained the lady. She was stout and elderly, her voice deep and patrician. "It's been working its way in for the best part of two years, and during that wet May we had it became quite serious. One sometimes feels one's fighting a losing battle."

There were damp patches around the crack and in the vault above it, and in the years since Pevsner had described it the plaster had lost its glare. You could see where it had been patched and repatched, too, and the nave as a whole was pervaded by a musty smell, like the odour of old, damp books.

"Actually, that crack looks quite promising..." murmured Clara, abstractedly patting the shoulder bag which she'd brought with her. She hadn't told me what was in it, except to say that it was "some stuff that might come in useful, you never know".

"Well, what do we do now?" I asked.

"Go see the Vicar, I suppose. The Reverend Cyprian Spencer, by the look of it," said Clara, reading from a list of incumbents set in a frame on the wall.

We asked the lady where he lived, and were told that the New Vicarage - "I call it 'New', but of course it's not, not really, though seventy years ago it was" - was at the other end of the village. "A 'thirties house, by itself. You can't miss it."

We didn't, and arrived there five minutes later.

"Yes?" said the man who opened the door. He was tall, thin, pale, quite young, and had an ascetic look about him - notwithstanding the frilly apron, lightly stained with egg and flour, that he was wearing. It was the dog collar that gave him away, however - he was the Reverend Spencer, no doubt.

"Have you a moment? We've come about the Church..." I said.

"The Church?"

There was a defensive note in his voice, as though he thought I meant the Church as a whole, and that we'd come to bring up some old doctrinal dispute or to give him an earful about the New Age. I quickly put him right.

"I mean St Martha's. You are the Vicar of St Martha's, aren't you?"

"Oh, St Martha's is just one of the Churches I look after," he said airily, making it sound as though, in addition to being a priest, he was a kind of all-round handyman.

"Well, could we have a word about St Martha's? It's just that we've found out something...well, rather interesting about it. At least, I'm sure it will be of interest to *you*," I said, though as a matter of fact I wasn't. The fellow in front of us wasn't one of your trendy vicars with an earring and a ponytail and a tendency to hug you if given half a chance. Rather, he was one of your High Church types, with an aquiline nose and a fondness for incense, cloaks and birettas. Also, judging by the way he was looking down said nose at my sister, he was taking a dim view of her appearance.

"Very well, you had better come in and introduce yourselves," he said finally. "But I can't give you much time. I'm expecting the Vicar of All Saints, Godstone, at any moment."

Removing his apron, he ushered us into a parlour containing a harpsichord, a great many books, a couple of Persian rugs, and an expensive three piece suite complete with leather pouffe. On graduating from Theological College, the Rev. Spencer must have decided that if he was going to be an ascetic, he was going to be one in style. We sat down on the settee and told him that there were important mediaeval murals beneath the plaster in St Martha's - or so we had good reason to believe.

The essence of it, from our point of view, was that we wanted him to set the wheels in motion. In other words, we wanted his eyes to light up at the mention of the murals and his mouth to start saying: "This is tremendous news, tremendous. O sing ye, sing ye praises to the Lord! St Martha's has been about to fall down for years, but if we can just uncover these murals, a government grant should be in the bag, etc, etc." Then, once he'd set the wheels in motion, we could go to the National Trust, tell them about the particular mural we hoped to uncover, and ask them to put their decision as to Quine's project on hold, at the very least.

However, the Vicar's eyes did not light up nor did his mouth come out with the above. Instead, his eyes grew narrower and his mouth ditto. He heard us out in silence, then said, or rather, pronounced - for he had one of those voices which made him sound as though he had a miniature church in his voicebox and was speaking from the far end of it:

"It does seem to me very unlikely - extremely unlikely, if I may say so - that these 'murals' still exist. If indeed they existed in the first place."

"Oh, they existed all right," said Clara impatiently. "And the point is this: your plaster needs redoing anyway, so why not strip it all off and have a proper look?"

"But, if they *were* there, which is, *eh-hem*, highly questionable, surely the plaster would have ruined them," he said disdainfully.

"On the contrary, it could have helped to preserve them. It's often the case," said Clara.

"And just think," I said, arguing *à la* Sohrab Quine, "If they *were* there, you'd be able to get some lottery money to do them up, no sweat."

"*And* you'd get your name in *The Church Times*," said Clara.

"Or even in **The Times**," I added.

"Pooh, these temporal considerations don't weigh with us. They simply don't weigh with us," replied the Vicar. His eyes were growing distinctly less narrow, though, I noticed. "Besides, I cannot just wave a magic wand and say 'Let this work be done because' - you'll forgive me for putting it like this, I'm sure - 'a couple of teenagers have told me it must be done'. No, no - oh, no, no, no. We would have to look at the evidence for your claims, that evidence would have to have a sound academic base, the Parish Council would have to be convened, I would have to talk with the Bishop, funds would have to be raised...and so on." He waved a pale, pianist's hand in a languid gesture to one side, as though to put the magic wand back in its drawer, unused. "Oh, and by the way, just what *is* your evidence for the existence of these murals?"

I was surprised that it had taken him so long to get round to the obvious question. The trouble was, though, that it wasn't only obvious, it was also jolly awkward. If we mentioned the Bastable manuscript, the chances were that sooner or later Bryan Mandeville would get to hear of it - and that could prove tricky, very tricky indeed. One could only imagine the searching questions he and his solicitors would ask. And though we might have answered them by claiming that the Bastable was our own copy, not his, I didn't really feel that that would wash. How many handwritten copies of the thing could there be? And what kind of story could we tell about where we'd got it from?

And yet, if we didn't tell the Rev. Spencer about the manuscript, how else were we to convince him?

Of course, Clara and I had discussed this little difficulty earlier, but we hadn't really come to a conclusion. And now here we were with a ticklish problem on our hands.

But that's youngsters for you, I guess. We'd gone and rushed in where angels would have feared to tread.

Meanwhile, the Vicar was waiting for an answer. So, I started to mumble something about a book, an old book - when Clara broke in with the following unexpected statement:

"I had a dream."

"I beg your pardon?" said the Vicar.

"A dream. I had a dream. Well, more of a vision, really."

There was a long pause after this.

"I see," said the Vicar coldly.

"She often has visions, don't you, Clara?" I said helpfully.

"Yes, quite often," said Clara.

178

"I see," said the Vicar in an even chillier voice.

"Yes, so do I. Or rather, so did I. In my vision, I mean. I saw the inside of your church, and there were these murals on the wall, and there was a picture of Woodcote Hill in one of them, and - " said Clara, warming to her theme, when the Reverend Spencer interrupted her.

"I think we have heard enough, Miss...whoever you are," he said, standing up and signalling to us to leave with a limp wave of his pale hand.

"But the murals are *there*. We're *sure* they are," I said desperately.

"So you have said," replied the Vicar with a thin smile.

And so we would have said again, I suppose, had not the doorbell rung and the Vicar of All Saints, Godstone, turned up for his supper.

The Revelation

It seemed to me strangely fitting, as we toiled back down the village street, that in addition to Dad's colleagues and Quine, plus the bureaucrats at the Heritage Department, the P.M., and for that matter the Smith-Enderbys (representing the world of Commerce), the Vicar had now thrown in his lot against us. Of course, we hadn't actually mentioned the Shiva figure and all of Dad's woes, but I was fairly certain in my own mind that not much good would have come from it if we had. Apart from not being a trendy vicar, the Reverend Cyprian Spencer had failed to strike me as being one of those C of E types who are keen on inter-faith get-togethers with Hindus, Muslims, Jains *et al*, and like to talk about our all having one Father, etc. The image of Shiva, I thought, would have been a bit too much for him to take, and had I broached the subject it would only have been to make him the more intractable.

So now we had a complete set of opponents, as it were - and this, as I say, seemed oddly satisfying. Though of no actual help, of course.

"I guess we could get a photocopy of the passage in Bastable and show him that," I suggested.

"It might work in the short term, but once the academics got hold of it, they'd want to know where it came from, and all the rest of it."

"Yeah, I suppose so. Anyway, where are we going?" I asked, for instead of turning left towards Woodcote Hill and home, Clara was leading us back to the Church.

"I just want to have a look at that crack again. If you don't mind."

I replied that I didn't mind, though I did have some homework which I'd have to do later, and thus we re-entered the Church. The lady who had been arranging the flowers was just leaving, and asked us if we would mind returning the key to the warden, two doors away, when we'd finished.

Clara took the key and watched the lady go down the path and out through the lych gate. Then she locked the door. I sat on a pew and wondered what was coming next.

First, she put her shoulder bag down on the font and took a sketchbook out of it. "In case we had to kill some time, waiting for other people to go," she explained. Then out came her camera, complete with flash unit. And, finally, a mallet and two of her sculptor's chisels.

I stood up. "Are you going to do what I think you're going to do?" I demanded.

"Yes, why not?" She pointed at the wall. "That crack just needs a little help, and a tap or two in the right place should do it. Besides, this plaster *needs* to come off."

"Yes, so you told the Vicar. But - "

"And anyway, there's a time for talking and there's a time for action. And it seems to me that the time for action has come."

And with that, she hoisted herself onto the nearest windowsill, stretched up and across, and started whacking away at the plaster. Like I said, in some ways she was a surprising girl.

But what happened next surprised us both.

At first I was full of trepidation. It appeared to me that, if anything was, this was a job for experts. What if, instead of revealing the mural, Clara broke it into pieces? Or what if the mural *was* revealed, but not the bit we wanted? Was she going start chipping away at the whole wall? Or what if the Vicar and his pal came along to have a look for themselves, while waiting for their wine to cool?

Yet none of these things happened. Instead, after tapping at an angle into the existing crack, Clara crossed over to the next window-sill and began to cut a second crack at a forty-five degree angle to the first, so that had both cracks been continued to the floor, they would have formed two sides of a triangle. Then, working with the kind of relish ascribed to Bernini, she tapped into this second crack with the chisel held almost flat against the wall. And the next thing we knew, there was a crumbling, rending sound, and a huge segment of plaster fell forward and toppled and sagged onto the floor.

"Phew!" I exclaimed, as the cloud of malodorous dust began to settle. And then -

"Good *grief!*"

For there in front of me was the picture that Bastable had described. Here and there it was still coated with whitewash, and here and there the painting itself had flaked off, being still attached to the plaster which now lay in a twisted swathe on the floor, half propped up on the bucket, and the whole image was covered with a thin white film - but that it was Bastable's picture there could be no doubt. In the foreground were Adam and Eve, behind them was the tree with a crudely drawn snake entwined round its trunk, and behind and above that was a hill with three spurs. And smack bang on the central spur, as clear as day and not damaged at all, was the great dancing image of Shiva, the Spirit. The clarity of the image was amazing, its significance incontrovertible. It was as though the god had used his own outstretched left foot to kick the plaster veil away and reveal this picture of himself, and the past, and a meaning which with the passage of time had been first neglected, then lost.

Clara laughed, and brushed the dust from her eyes, her mouth, her hair.

And Afterwards

And that, more or less, was that. Armed with the photos which Clara had taken of our find and his unpublished book, Dad went to see the gang who run the National Trust with a new confidence, a new sense of authority. And did they listen to him?

They did.

And were they pleased?

They were.

For, although for appearance's sake they had been prepared to go along with Quine's project, it seemed that in their heart of hearts they hadn't been too enamoured of the thought of fixing up a well-known beauty spot with a gigantic image of a bloke who, while he could just about rhyme 'baby' with 'maybe', was not exactly the new Bob Dylan, and whose music, when played at the recommended volume, had been scientifically proved to numb the limbic area of the brain, quite apart from what it did to your hearing. And so, now that they had some real, hard evidence of the Shiva image, they were quite happy to reinstate it.

And that, they believed, would scotch any other attempts to cut pop icons on the Surrey Hills, for to do such a thing when the image of Shiva was being recarved there would speak of a lack of originality - and to be seen to be short of originality was the one thing no artist desired.

One can imagine that when he heard of their decision, Sohrab Quine was none too pleased. At any rate, he wrote a stinging letter to *Studio International* and lodged an appeal at the National Trust H.Q. No sooner had he done this, however, than he was overtaken by events - for after another big bust-up with his brother Tycho, Ronnie Bastard decided to quit The Complete Bastards and tear up his recording contract into the bargain. His record company, aggrieved that The Bastards' last big hit had not been as big as their first or second or third big hits, and forewarned by their A & R boys that Ronnie's next release, a solo concept album, was a genuine turkey, said: "Okay, you're free - but we get to keep your name and logo, as they were thought up by the whizzkids in our Creative Department and they're our intellectual property." In turn, Ronnie decided that he'd now be known as 'The Artist Who Used To Be Called Something Else', and as for the logo, he disowned it.

Which all had the effect of throwing Quine's project into disarray. Ronnie Bastard without his name and logo was somehow not the same as Ronnie Bastard with them, and to push ahead with the image now might have made Quine look as though he were taking the side of the fat cats in the corporation against the lonely individual artist, etc., etc.

You may wonder about the Vicar. Wasn't he a trifle suspicious when he was told that, five minutes after having first been alerted to the fact that there were murals hidden in his church, the murals themselves had appeared?

Well, all I can say is that if he was, we never got to hear of it. On the contrary, he seemed, if anything, rather chuffed

- for a few weeks later, idly flipping through a copy of the Hookland Parish Magazine in my dentist's waiting room, I noticed an article by Cyprian Spencer, Vicar, written in order to celebrate the award of £100,000 of lottery cash to his church for the restoration of their mediaeval murals.

Entitled *Miracle At St Martha's*, it described how he'd been 'visited by a bright-haired angel, speaking in a strange tongue of painted images' just seconds before the plaster had dropped off the wall, revealing them.

And what of Bryan Mandeville? Fed up to the back teeth with the turn that things had taken, he put his house on the market and went off for a long holiday - and I can't say I was surprised. To have continued to live next door to the reminder of his failure would have been too a hard pill for most villains to swallow. Oh, and he chucked in his job as well. But don't worry, there's a rumour going around the Ancient History circuit that he's thinking of entering a new field, one in which his personality will at last have the scope to express itself. That's right. Politics.

We still returned the Bastable manuscript to its cubby-hole in the grotto, however, just to be on the safe side. You never knew. He might have come back from his hols with the suspicion that, somewhere along the line, there had been some fishy business involved. Therefore it seemed best to tidy up all the loose ends.

As for Mandeville's job, the vacancy has just been offered to Dad. He may take it up, but somehow I doubt it. Like Clara, he's considering his options. For one thing, his book is going to be published. For another, a TV documentary about the finding of the Chalk Giant is going to be produced, with a commentary by Dad. He's done some preliminary work for it already, and the bosses at Broadcasting House like his style. Apparently, he has just the right sort of mild eccentricity which comes across well on TV. So, they're talking of doing a series with Dad as a guide to the ancient sites of Britain...and after that, who knows? Perhaps a series on the ancient sites of the world.

Of course, we told him the whole story of the letter, the tracking down of the manuscript, and the stripping away of the plaster; and not only was he suitably impressed, he was also deeply moved. You could see a peacefulness spread over him as he looked at his family - we were sitting in the garden at the time on a warm June night, Vega shining brightly in the heavens above us and the white nicotianas in the border beside us in their own way resembling stars - and you could see a joyfulness well up in him, too, as he saw that his dream of the recarving of the Shiva figure was going to be fulfilled.

What more is there to say? Just this, perhaps. The other evening I walked onto Woodcote Hill and looked out over the Weald to the South Downs. A father and son were flying a kite. A stranger out walking her dog greeted me. A girl with a sketch pad under her arm smiled as she passed by. And as I gazed across the fields and woods, over Reigate and Hookland and Betchworth and the mistier, more distant villages, the feeling that we had won a true victory arose and grew in me. Of course, I'd felt triumphant from the moment that the National Trust had vetoed Quine's idea and given Dad's the go-ahead, but now all of a sudden I saw our achievement in a detached, impersonal way - and yes, it really was a victory. For it seemed that the powers that be, the ruling powers, the maleficent powers of bad art, the powers of inertia and envy and money, had all done their worst, and yet, over all the fair land before me, the image of the Spirit was going to prevail. I felt a sense of hope, of exuberant expectancy. And in that mood I turned for home.

Printed in the United States
65623LVS00001BB/57